I0609437

Love's Harvest

A Lilac Lake Book

by

Judith Keim

Wild Quail Publishing

BOOKS BY JUDITH KEIM

THE HARTWELL WOMEN SERIES:

The Talking Tree – 1
Sweet Talk – 2
Straight Talk – 3
Baby Talk – 4
The Hartwell Women – Boxed Set

THE BEACH HOUSE HOTEL SERIES:

Breakfast at The Beach House Hotel – 1
Lunch at The Beach House Hotel – 2
Dinner at The Beach House Hotel – 3
Christmas at The Beach House Hotel – 4
Margaritas at The Beach House Hotel – 5
Dessert at The Beach House Hotel – 6
Coffee at The Beach House Hotel – 7
High Tea at The Beach House Hotel – 8
Nightcaps at The Beach House Hotel – 9
Bubbles at The Beach House Hotel – 10
Canapes at The Beach House Hotel – 11 (2025)
Sea Breezes at The Beach House Hotel – 12 (2026)

THE FAT FRIDAYS GROUP:

Fat Fridays – 1
Sassy Saturdays – 2
Secret Sundays – 3

THE SALTY KEY INN SERIES:

Finding Me – 1

Finding My Way – 2

Finding Love – 3

Finding Family – 4

The Salty Key Inn Series – Boxed Set

SEASHELL COTTAGE BOOKS:

A Christmas Star

Change of Heart

A Summer of Surprises

A Road Trip to Remember

The Beach Babes

THE CHANDLER HILL INN SERIES:

Going Home – 1

Coming Home – 2

Home at Last – 3

The Chandler Hill Inn Series – Boxed Set

THE DESERT SAGE INN SERIES:

The Desert Flowers – Rose – 1

The Desert Flowers – Lily – 2

The Desert Flowers – Willow – 3

The Desert Flowers – Mistletoe & Holly – 4

The Desert Sage Inn Series – Boxed Set

SOUL SISTERS AT CEDAR MOUNTAIN LODGE:

Christmas Sisters – Anthology
Christmas Kisses
Christmas Castles
Christmas Stories – Soul Sisters Anthology
Christmas Joy
The Christmas Joy Boxed Set

THE SANDERLING COVE INN SERIES:

Waves of Hope – 1
Sandy Wishes – 2
Salty Kisses – 3

THE LILAC LAKE INN SERIES

Love by Design – 1
Love Between the Lines – 2
Love Under the Stars – 3

LILAC LAKE BOOKS

Love's Cure
Love's Home Run
Love's Bloom – (2025)
Love's Harvest – (2025)
Love's Match – (2026)

OTHER BOOKS:

The ABCs of Living With a Dachshund
Trouble At The Winston Hotel... a Mouse Mystery
Holiday Hopes
The Winning Tickets

For more information: **www.judithkeim.com**

PRAISE FOR JUDITH KEIM'S NOVELS

THE BEACH HOUSE HOTEL SERIES – Books 1 – 12:

"Love the characters in this series. This series was my first introduction to Judith Keim. She is now one of my favorites. Looking forward to reading more of her books."

BREAKFAST AT THE BEACH HOUSE HOTEL – *"An easy, delightful read that offers romance, family relationships, and strong women learning to be stronger. Real life situations filter through the pages. Enjoy!"*

LUNCH AT THE BEACH HOUSE HOTEL – *"This series is such a joy to read. You feel you are actually living with them. Can't wait to read the latest one."*

DINNER AT THE BEACH HOUSE HOTEL – *"A Terrific Read! As usual, Judith Keim did it again. Enjoyed immensely. Continue writing such pleasantly reading books for all of us readers."*

CHRISTMAS AT THE BEACH HOUSE HOTEL – *"Not Just Another Christmas Novel. This is book number four in the series and my introduction to Judith Keim's writing. I wasn't disappointed. The characters are dimensional and engaging. The plot is well crafted and advances at a pleasing pace.*

MARGARITAS AT THE BEACH HOUSE HOTEL – *"Overall, Margaritas at the Beach House Hotel is another wonderful addition to the series. Judith Keim takes the reader on a journey told through the voices of these amazing characters we have all come to love through the years!*

DESSERT AT THE BEACH HOUSE HOTEL – *"It is a heartwarming and beautiful women's fiction as only Judith Keim can do with her wonderful characters, amazing location. and family and friends whose daily lives circle around Ann and Rhonda and The Beach House Hotel.*

COFFEE AT THE BEACH HOUSE HOTEL – *"Great story and characters! A hard to put down book. Lots of things happening, including a kidnapping of a young boy. The beach house hotel is a wonderful hotel run by two women who are best friends. Highly recommend this book.*

HIGH TEA AT THE BEACH HOUSE HOTEL – *"What a lovely story! The Beach House Hotel series is always a great read. Each book in the series brings a new aspect to the saga of Ann and Rhonda."*

THE HARTWELL WOMEN SERIES – Books 1 – 4:

"This was an EXCELLENT series. When I discovered Judith Keim, I read all of her books back to back. I thoroughly enjoyed the women Keim has written about. They are believable and you want to just jump into their lives and be their friends! I can't wait for any upcoming books!"

"I fell into Judith Keim's Hartwell Women series and have read & enjoyed all of her books in every series. Each centers around a strong & interesting woman character and their family interaction. Good reads that leave you wanting more."

THE FAT FRIDAYS GROUP – Books 1 – 3:

"Excellent story line for each character, and an insightful representation of situations which deal with some of the contemporary issues women are faced with today."

THE SALTY KEY INN SERIES – Books 1 – 4:

FINDING ME – *"The characters are endearing with the same struggles we all encounter. The setting makes me feel like I am a guest at The Salty Key Inn...relaxed, happy & light-hearted! The men are yummy and the women strong. You can't get better than that! Happy Reading!"*

FINDING MY WAY- *"Loved the family dynamics as well as uncertain emotions of dating and falling in love. Appreciated the morals and strength of parenting throughout. Just couldn't put this book down."*

FINDING LOVE – *"Judith Keim always puts substance into her books. This book was no different, I learned about PTSD, accepting oneself, there are always going to be problems but stick it out and make it work.*

FINDING FAMILY – *"Completing this series is like eating the last chip. Love Judith's writing and her female characters are always smart, strong, vulnerable to life and love experiences."*

"This was a refreshing book. Bringing the heart and soul of the family to us."

THE CHANDLER HILL INN SERIES – Books 1 – 3:

GOING HOME – *"I was completely immersed in this book, with the beautiful descriptive writing, and the author's way of bringing her characters to life. I felt like I was right inside her story."*

COMING HOME – *"Coming Home was such a wonderful story. The author has such a gift for getting the reader right to the heart of things."*

HOME AT LAST – *"In this wonderful conclusion, to a heartfelt and emotional trilogy set in Oregon's stunning wine country, Judith Keim has tied up the Chandler Hill series with the perfect bow."*

SEASHELL COTTAGE BOOKS:

A CHRISTMAS STAR – *"Love, laughter, sadness, great food, and hope for the future, all in one book. It doesn't get any better than this stunning read."*

CHANGE OF HEART – *"CHANGE OF HEART is the summer read we've all been waiting for. Judith Keim is a master at creating fascinating characters that are simply irresistible. Her stories leave you with a big smile on your face and a heart bursting with love."*
~Kellie Coates Gilbert, author of the popular Sun Valley Series

A SUMMER OF SURPRISES – *"Ms. Keim uses this book as an amazing platform to show that with hard emotional work, belief in yourself, and love, the scars of abuse can be conquered. It in no way preaches, it's a lovely story with a happy ending."*

A ROAD TRIP TO REMEMBER – *"The characters are so real that they jump off the page. Such a fun, HAPPY book at the perfect time. It will lift your spirits and even remind you of your own grandmother. Spirited and hopeful Aggie gets a second chance at love and she takes the steering wheel and drives straight for it."*

THE BEACH BABES – *"Another winner at the pen of Judith Keim. I love the characters and the book just flows. It feels as though you are at the beach with them and are a part of you.*

THE DESERT SAGE INN SERIES – Books 1 – 4:

THE DESERT FLOWERS – ROSE – *"The Desert Flowers - Rose, "In this first of a series, we see each woman come into her own and view new beginnings even as they must take this tearful journey as they slowly lose a dear friend.*

THE DESERT FLOWERS – LILY – *"The second book in the Desert Flowers series is just as wonderful as the first. Judith Keim is a brilliant storyteller. Her characters are truly lovely and people that you want to be friends with as soon as you start reading. Judith Keim is not afraid to weave real-life conflict and loss into her stories.*

THE DESERT FLOWERS – WILLOW – *"The feelings of love, joy, happiness, friendship, family, and the pain of loss are deeply felt by Willow Sanchez and her two cohorts Rose and Lily. The Desert Flowers met because of their deep feelings for Alec Thurston, a man who touched their lives in different ways."*

MISTLETOE AND HOLLY – *"As always, the author never ceases to amaze me. She's able to take characters and bring them to life in such a way that you think you're actually among family. It's a great holiday read. You won't be disappointed."*

THE SANDERLING COVE INN SERIES

WAVES OF HOPE – "Such a wonderful story about several families in a beautiful location in Florida. A grandmother requests her three granddaughters to help her by running the family's inn for the summer. Other grandmothers in the area played a part in this plan to find happiness for their grandsons and granddaughters."

SANDY WISHES – *"Three cousins needing a change and a few of the neighborhood boys from when they were young are back visiting their grandmothers. It is an adventure, a summer of discoveries, and embracing the person they are becoming."*

SALTY KISSES – *"I love this story, as well as the entire series because it's about family, friendship, and love. The meddling grandmothers have only the best intentions and want to see their grandchildren find love and happiness. What grandparent wouldn't want that?"*

THE LILAC LAKE INN SERIES – Books 1 – 3:

LOVE BY DESIGN –"Genie Wittner is planning on selling her beloved Lilac Inn B&B, and keeping a cottage for her three granddaughters, Whitney, the movie star, Dani an architect, and Taylor a writer. A little mystery, a possible ghost, and romance all make this a great read and the start of a new series."

LOVE BETWEEN THE LINES – "Taylor is one of 3 sisters who have inherited a cottage in Lilac Lake from their grandmother. She is an accomplished author who is having some issues getting inspired for her next book. Things only get worse when she receives an email from her new editor with a harsh critique of her last book. She's still fuming when Cooper shows up in town, determined to work together on getting the book ready."

LOVE UNDER THE STARS – "Love Under the Stars is the third book in The Lilac Lake Inn Series by author Judith Keim. Judith beautifully weaves together the final story in this amazing series about the Gilford sisters and their grandmother, GG."

THE LILAC LAKE BOOKS

LOVE'S CURE – Welcome back to Lilac Lake with a new spin-off series from author Judith Keim. For fans of the author, you will be reunited with previous characters, as well as being introduced to new ones. Even though this book can be read as a stand-alone, I highly recommend reading the Lilac Lake Inn series to get introduced to all of these amazing characters.

Love's Harvest

A Lilac Lake Book

by

Judith Keim

Wild Quail Publishing

Love's Harvest is a work of fiction. Names, characters, places, public or private institutions, corporations, towns, and incidents are the product of the author's imagination or are used fictitiously. Any resemblance to actual events, locales, or persons, living or dead, is coincidental.

No part of *Love's Harvest* may be reproduced or transmitted in any form or by any electronic or mechanical means, including information storage and retrieval systems, without permission in writing from the author, except by a reviewer who may quote brief passages in a review. This book may not be resold or uploaded for distribution to others. For permissions, contact the author directly via electronic mail:

wildquail.pub@gmail.com
www.judithkeim.com

Wild Quail Publishing
PO Box 171332
Boise, ID 83717-1332

ISBN 978-1-962452-89-2
Copyright ©2025, Judith Keim
All rights reserved

Dedication

For those who give comfort to others who need it.

CHAPTER ONE

***Heart pounding, she raced into the South Carolina** woods, smashing dried leaves beneath her feet, struggling to catch her breath, intent on finding her husband. The farther she went, the sicker she felt. Suddenly she stopped and grabbed onto her sides.*

Ahead, a figure was sprawled on the ground.

She drew closer, then let out a bloodcurdling scream as she stared at the mixture of blood, skin, and bone that remained of his head. "No-o-o, Jesse, No-o-o!"

Sarah Bullard Miller bolted up from her bed with a start and drew a deep breath. Then another. She rubbed her eyes and reminded herself this was just a dream of something awful that had happened two years ago.

She sat quietly and listened, hoping her two daughters hadn't heard her cries.

All was quiet.

Her adrenaline left her in a rush, leaving her feeling weak and nauseous. The dream was always the same, followed by a familiar pattern of emotions, everything from anger to a sense of loss to guilt. Suicide survivors told similar stories, and though it was helpful to know she wasn't alone in feeling this way, it didn't lessen her sense of failure.

Weary, she got up out of bed and wandered into the

kitchen of the riverside cabin she was renting in her hometown of Lilac Lake, New Hampshire. She looked out at the pinkening streaks in the sky that indicated another pleasant fall day. Feeling more grounded, Sarah fixed herself a cup of coffee and took a seat at the kitchen table, trying to settle her nerves. The nightmare wasn't as frequent a visitor as it had been at the beginning. Therapy and being back home, where she helped her parents with the Bullard's Hardware Store, were all part of her plan to try to get back to a healthier life with her four-year-old twin daughters, Mia and Emily.

She heard the girls moving about in their bedroom and watched as they padded into the kitchen, climbed up into her lap, and sleepily laid their heads on her shoulders. Out of the wreckage of the past, these were her treasures. She adored them. At four, the girls were active and always doing something. What one didn't think of for getting into trouble, the other did. Emily's hair was light-brown, while Mia's was a bit blonder. But all four eyes were the same distracting green color in identical faces — faces with classic features like their father's.

"Do we have school again today?" asked Emily.

"I like school," Mia said.

"That's helpful because you're going to school like you usually do, so I can help Mimi and PopPop at the store."

A while later, Sarah left her girls at their preschool while she continued her walk to work. It was convenient living in the center of the small town in the Lakes Region of New Hampshire. She could walk to most places.

She'd grown up in Lilac Lake, never appreciating the

striking beauty of the town with its cute, colorful shops and restaurants along Main Street, the white-steepled church, and the town common where summer concerts and other town events were held. Standing in the middle of the town overlooking the common was Bullard's Hardware Store, her parents' establishment, and her place of employment.

Now, as she strolled through town, she stopped and looked into the windows of The Wild Flower Boutique, displaying many beautiful pieces of clothing. Next door, Pages Book Store held an enticing display of new releases. Mixed in among the retail shops were several cafes and Jake's bar, where a lot of people her age met regularly.

Sarah moved along the street, admiring the colorful fall flowers planted in huge planters flanking the doors of many of the shops. Some, like the Artists Collaborative, flew the American flag. At this time of year, baskets of marigolds hung from the decorative lamp posts that lined the Main Street shopping area. But when Halloween arrived, the posts would be wrapped with black and orange ribbons. At Christmas, they would display holiday wreaths and twinkling white lights.

Feeling a warm sense of being back home, she saw her high school boyfriend, Aaron Collister, emerge from beneath the purple awning of the Lilac Lake Café carrying a cup filled with coffee, no doubt. She paused to study him.

He turned and gazed at her with those dark brown, almost black eyes that had captured her attention growing up. His straight dark hair was tied behind his head. After all that had gone on with her marriage and life in South Carolina, she still felt drawn to him, an almost spiritual pull.

Aaron stilled. Then he acknowledged her with a bob of his head before his two black Labs barked to get into his truck, diverting his attention.

Sarah went on her way filled with such sadness for all she couldn't change that she couldn't hold back the mistiness that blurred her vision. She had so much to be grateful for, and so many regrets.

Sarah walked into the store, which had always seemed like a colorful wonderland to her, filled with everything a family might need, from a certain screw to the latest kitchen utensil. When she was little, she'd thought the store at Christmas was a special, magical place just for her.

Her father, tall and gray-haired, stood at the cash register, getting it set up for the day.

"Hi, sweetie," he said. "I bought you a cup of coffee and a scone at the café. It's sitting on your desk."

"Thanks, Dad," Sarah said. It was both sweet and annoying to be pampered by him. She loved both of her parents, but she sometimes felt as if she'd slipped back into high school, and the intervening years had been just a bad dream.

Sarah climbed the stairs to the second floor, which held her office and her mother's, and was also where some of the home décor and gift items were stored. Larger items, such as kitchen appliances, hand and electric tools, and landscaping equipment and supplies, were stored in the back of the first floor, near the loading dock. People who'd never been employed in a large, regional hardware store and garden shop had no idea of the work involved in keeping the store filled with the right merchandise. She loved overseeing the garden shop during the spring and summer, and the holiday shop for

Halloween, Christmas, and other holidays.

"Your dad bought you coffee and a scone," her mother said as Sarah walked by her office.

"Yes, I know," said Sarah, moving into her own office. Not much got past her mother. Sometimes it felt suffocating.

Sarah sat in her chair, picked up the coffee cup, and took a long, satisfying sip. That warmth, along with the promise of a new day, always energized her.

Her mother came into the office and handed her a bunch of invoices. "I need these checked over and then entered into the computer. I see you're ordering more items for Halloween."

"I'm planning for our store to be a stop on the annual Halloween Trick-or-Treat Walk for the kids in town."

"Great idea," said her mother, smiling. Her mother was a pleasant woman who didn't like conflict, which is one reason her parents were such a strong couple. She'd always fussed about Sarah's weight growing up. Now, it wasn't a problem. The energy required to work and raise her two active daughters was keeping Sarah's weight under control. Not that Sarah cared.

Her mother sat down in a chair facing Sarah's desk. "I heard that the Gilford women are having a party this Saturday at their Lilac Lake cottage. Will you be going? If so, I can take care of the girls."

"Thanks. I'd like to go and see the gang. It's very special that so many of my friends have either remained in town or returned after college."

"No matter how things have turned out for you, I'm glad you went to college and got your business degree. Having you here is such a help to your father and me. It's always been a dream of ours to be able to hand the business over to you someday."

"I know," Sarah said, taking hold of the scone. She could already feel her spirits plummet, and she needed a bit of sugar. She loved the idea of taking over the store, but she needed more time to recover from her husband's death before she could put real energy behind it. Or into life itself.

Later, those gloomy thoughts evaporated as she dug into her work. She enjoyed dealing with numbers; they were predictable. However, she also had a creative streak, which she loved even more.

Her cell phone rang. *Crystal.*

Smiling, she clicked on the call. Crystal Owens, now Crystal Chambers, was married to Emmett Chambers, the GP in town, and was very sweet about checking in with her from time to time. Especially if she hadn't joined her friends in the group of locals her age at Jake's bar in a while.

"Hey, girlfriend, I just wanted to make sure you knew about the party on Saturday at the Lilac Lake Cottage. All three Gilford sisters will be in town, and they wanted me to make sure you could come. We know how hard it is for you sometimes to get away."

"My mother has already promised to babysit, so I'm free to be there. Thanks so much. What's going on with you?"

"I'm continuing to work in Emmett's medical office, and I'm really liking it. In addition to reception and office work, I'm helping with his patients. With the opening of the Emergency Center and with the number of people, both elderly and young, needing time to discuss their problems, I'm finding it very interesting to help them come up with solutions. Nothing beyond simple, logical solutions. But

Emmett is thrilled with the response he's getting from my participation."

"Having accessible medical help in rural areas is a problem for so many states. I'm very relieved he chose to stay in Lilac Lake," Sarah said.

"Me, too. How are those adorable girls of yours?" Crystal asked, and Sarah noted a tinge of envy in her voice.

"They're doing really well. They love it here. Having my parents involved in their lives has been very special."

"And how are you doing?" Crystal asked quietly. "It's been just over a year since you returned to Lilac Lake."

"I'm slowly healing," Sarah said. "Since my husband's death, I've been seeing a grief counselor, and she's helped me a lot. As much as anyone could." She hadn't admitted even to Crystal that she couldn't think of herself as worthy of a man's love again. She hadn't been able to do enough to save her husband.

Crystal broke into the silence. "Recovering from someone's suicide is a shattering thing for anyone to handle. Please don't try to do it alone."

"In this town?" joked Sarah.

Crystal laughed. "I'm so glad you haven't lost your sense of humor. You were always such fun to be around growing up."

"I'm trying," Sarah said honestly. "Thanks for the call. See you Saturday."

After they finished talking, Sarah sat for a moment, remembering her high school days when she was the one everyone wanted to include because of her upbeat, smiling, laughing manner. If only she could become that person again.

###

Sarah left the store and went to pick up the girls from preschool. She was lucky that Cherie Downes, a former kindergarten teacher in town, had decided to open a preschool, "Bright Beginnings," for a limited number of children. Not everyone who applied for the program was accepted. Sarah had endured a long interview process about her philosophy on raising children and how much quality time she was able to spend with her girls. She'd passed with flying colors.

Mia and Emily were thrilled that Cherie's two teenage daughters helped out from time to time. Already, the twins were fussy about what clothes they wanted to wear. Thankfully, they didn't want to dress alike. Sarah had gone out of her way to encourage them to avoid that routine.

When Sarah arrived at Bright Beginnings, other mothers were picking up their children. Sarah waved at them but didn't take the time to talk. She was anxious to get home. She'd left her cabin in a mess and wanted to have things in order in case Misty Owens or Hazel Belmont decided to drop by. She'd heard about the cabin for rent through Crystal's sister, Misty, and had jumped at the opportunity. She could easily walk to the preschool and to work from there.

When she entered the building, her two little girls ran to her.

"Mommy! Mommy!" they cried together.

Mia held up a paper with the letter "C" on it. "I colored it."

"Me, too," said Emily, not to be left out.

"We'll hang them on the bulletin board," Sarah said,

accepting the artwork. She kept a bulletin board in the kitchen where their art projects rotated from one to the next.

"Mine first," said Emily, smiling at her sister.

Mia shrugged, not taking the bait for a battle.

Sarah didn't interfere. She let them work out as many issues as possible on their own, but kept a close eye on them so that things remained equal between them.

On the walk home, the girls chattered about their day at school. Sarah smiled, listening to them. Having been an only child, she had longed for a sister, so seeing her two girls together now brought her happiness.

When they entered the cabin, Sarah silently scolded herself for being such a late riser. They'd left in a hurry as usual, and things were chaotic, with beds unmade and dirty dishes in the sink.

She gave the girls a snack, quickly straightened up, and started a load of laundry. As she worked, she glanced out the windows several times. The woods leading to the river were filled with birds chirping happily. She noticed a couple of squirrels running across the grass and knew they were busy storing nuts for the winter.

When Sarah had dated Aaron in high school, he'd made her aware of the wildlife around them, and she'd learned how to identify different birds from their appearance and their songs. One reason she loved living in the woods was because of Aaron and all he'd taught her to enjoy in nature. With leaves changing color, it was a gift.

Her parents had insisted on installing a fence in the backyard so the girls could play outside. Although Sarah wanted them to feel free, she understood the danger of the nearby river.

Sarah had talked to her counselor about this very issue. She had to be wise and practical, but she knew she couldn't become overly protective of the girls because she hadn't been able to help her husband deal with the depression he'd struggled with for so long.

The doorbell rang, and Sarah hurried to answer it. Living in the same group of cabins as two of her friends gave her easy opportunities to spend time with them.

She opened the door to find Misty Owens standing next to Hazel Belmont. They both taught at the local elementary school. Though she'd known Misty for years, Hazel was new to her. Originally from a town outside New Orleans, her soft, southern accent was charming.

"Come on in. I've put the kettle on for tea, unless you'd like something stronger. I have a nice rosé, which my mother discovered a couple of months ago."

"Wine sounds perfect," said Misty.

"Yeah, it's been a tough day," Hazel said. "I thought I'd love teaching, but it's much harder than I'd thought."

"It's exhausting, but I love it," said Misty. Whereas Crystal was a pretty, pale blonde, her sister, Misty, had dark hair and olive skin. Crystal had watched over Misty from a young age when their own addicted mother couldn't. Misty had left town and then returned after an abusive relationship. Now, she was happily in love with David Graham, who owned Graham Landscaping in town with his father.

Hazel was athletic and active, but she couldn't shake the southern belle impression with her slow, sugary speech, long brown hair pulled back into a ponytail, and her pants and frilly blouse molding to her long-legged, model's body.

The girls rushed over to greet them.

Tired or not, both women greeted them warmly, asking questions about their day.

Once the three adults were sitting in the kitchen, they relaxed with a glass of wine. "Are you going to the party on Saturday?" Misty asked Sarah.

"Yes. My mother is taking the girls for me, so I can come and go as I wish."

"It's nice to start the fall off with a get-together," said Hazel.

"There's no better place to do that than at the Lilac Lake Cottage. It used to be in terrible shape, but the three Gilford sisters have turned it into a stunning place," said Misty.

"I remember the Gilford girls when they were little. They spent every summer here so they could be here with their grandmother," said Sarah.

"Their grandmother owned the Lilac Lake Inn for years and recently sold it to an investment group, including Ross Roberts," Misty explained to Hazel. "The three Gilford women inherited the cottage with the agreement to fix it up and to occupy it for at least six months of the year. That's why Taylor stays there for as long as she can. Not a bad rule to have to follow,"

"I heard Taylor will be staying a few weeks while she's working on a new book," said Sarah. "Her husband, Cooper, will come from New York City as often as possible. But it gives us women a better chance of getting together with her if she's here alone."

"It's so cool to think we have an author in our midst," Hazel said.

"We have an interesting group of people our age in town," Misty added.

"By the way, I saw Aaron Collister this morning from across the street," said Sarah.

"The last time we were all at Jake's together, I tried to get him interested in me," admitted Hazel. "He's such a sweet man."

"But?' asked Sarah.

"He was very polite but not interested," said Hazel. "I hope some new people come to town because most of the decent single men are taken."

"I thought you and Mike Dawson were interested in one another," said Misty. Mike Dawson was a respected tennis player who'd opened the new Sports Center in town with Ross Roberts, the well-known former professional baseball player, who was also part-owner of the Lilac Lake Inn.

Hazel shook her head. "He's got someone in Florida who works at his tennis camp."

"Something will work out," said Sarah. She'd never admit it to anyone, but she was glad Aaron didn't fall for Hazel. Though nothing would come of it, she still liked how close she felt to him. But maybe that was being selfish on her part. And, heaven knew, he deserved someone much better.

After sitting and chatting for a while, Hazel said, "Anybody going to Jake's for supper? I want to see if Gabe is working. He's someone I could go for."

"I'm not going," said Misty. "I have to correct some test papers for my students. But, Sarah, if you want to go, I can correct the papers here and watch the girls for you. Now that my precious Sugar has died, I don't have to get home to take care of a dog anymore." Her eyes filled.

"I'm so sorry," said Sarah, giving her a hug. "I know how much you loved her."

"Thanks," said Misty. "I still miss her." She'd adopted a dog from a woman at The Woodlands assisted living facility. "But you two go ahead with your plans."

"What do you say, Sarah?" asked Hazel. "Shall we go? We don't have to stay late."

"Are you sure you don't mind, Misty? asked Sarah.

"Go, get out of the house, have fun. David already told me he won't be there."

At first, Misty and David had seemed an unlikely match, but after seeing them together and their growing love for one another, Sarah thought they were one of the sweetest couples in town.

"Okay, then I'll join you, Hazel. Let me make sure supper is ready. How do you like spaghetti, Misty?"

"It sounds delicious," said Misty. "This will give me the opportunity to spend some time alone with your daughters. I love kids their age."

"See?" said Hazel. "She's a born teacher."

"You'll find it easier," Misty told Hazel. "It takes time to learn a few of the tricks."

Sarah went to the girls' room to tell them about the change in plans.

"Hooray!" they cried, racing to the kitchen to find Misty.

"Guess they don't mind at all," said Sarah, chuckling. "Even so, I won't be gone long." She kissed each girl, picked up her purse, and left the house with Hazel.

Outside, Hazel turned to her. "It'll be nice to spend some time with you."

"For me, too," said Sarah, wishing she'd taken time to

brush her hair. Hazel always looked so put together.

"Let's walk," said Hazel. "I need the exercise."

"Fine with me," said Sarah. One benefit of being back in Lilac Lake was her ability to walk everywhere. It always made her feel healthy.

"So, what's the deal with you and Aaron? I know he likes you," said Hazel. "And it's easy to see you're attracted to him."

"He and I were high school sweethearts. If I hadn't gone away to college and met my husband, who knows what might have happened with us. Now, as much as I care for him, I won't let our friendship be more than that."

"For heaven's sake, why?" asked Hazel, giving her a steady look.

"Because of my husband," Sarah said quietly. "But I don't want to talk about it. Not ever."

Hazel held up a hand at the firmness in Sarah's voice. "Okay, I won't."

"Thanks," said Sarah. She'd discussed the situation with a counselor, but she didn't want to talk about it outside that room. It hurt too much.

CHAPTER TWO

WHEN SARAH AND HAZEL STEPPED INSIDE JAKE'S, THEY were greeted with the hum of conversation and the sound of sports games blaring from the televisions placed around the wood-paneled interior.

In the back corner of the main room, two large tables were usually reserved for the locals. Sarah and her friends made use of those tables, especially in the summer when it was the place to connect with other young adults. Even though many of the group were either married or engaged, it was still a spot where people liked to meet.

In many ways, Lilac Lake had become a young peoples' town. Friends Sarah had gone to high school with now served as leaders in local government positions, owned stores and other businesses, and took part in daily life here.

Sarah waved to Damon Pritchard, the new part owner of Jake's, behind the bar. His uncle, Jake Pritchard, had retired and left half the business to Damon and half to his son, Jake Jr., JayJay. Like his cousin, Damon had butterscotch hair, blue eyes, and an easy grin. Sarah wasn't able to back it up with actual numbers, but she swore that since the two young men were operating the bar, business had doubled. At least with female customers.

As they approached the corner tables, Sarah was delighted to see all three Gilford sisters with their significant others. The oldest of the three, Whitney, was there with her husband, Nick Woodruff, the chief of police, awaiting the birth of their second child. Dani, the other sister who lived in town, was married to Brad Collister and worked with him at The Meadows upscale housing development, along with Aaron. Taylor, the author, was married to Cooper Walker, an editor in a New York publishing house.

"Hello, everyone," said Sarah, beaming at the sisters. "I'm so glad to see you." She gave each woman a quick hug and greeted their spouses.

"It's always nice to see your beautiful smiling face," said Whitney. "I was thinking about you earlier and how much fun we all had during the summers."

"Yes, those were such special times for me," Sarah said, forcing herself to continue smiling. There was no going back to those days.

While Hazel was talking to Taylor about her latest book, Sarah took a seat next to Whitney.

Aaron approached the group and caught Sarah's eye before quickly sitting in the empty chair beside her.

She told herself that the warmth coursing through her was from the walk from her house to the bar, not from the look he was giving her.

Aaron's dark gaze rested on her, and he said quietly, "Nice to see you here. How are the girls?"

"Active as ever," she said.

"My offer to take them apple picking is still on," he said. "This is a perfect time of year to be outdoors with them."

"Thanks. Maybe we can work something out for Sunday. I'll be at the store all day on Saturday." Though she'd decided not to get too close to Aaron, she could never deny her children the chance for him to teach them about the outdoors he knew and loved. They'd missed so much by lacking a man's presence in their lives, except for their busy grandfather. When the girls' father was suffering through a bout of depression, he'd wanted nothing to do with them.

Soon, the number of occupants at the tables grew.

Ross Roberts, the ex-baseball star and part owner of the Lilac Lake Inn, arrived with a woman Sarah hadn't met before.

"Hey, everyone. This is Tessa Thorne, the new social director at the Lilac Lake Inn. I thought she should meet the people in our group, people about her same age."

Tessa was tall and thin with long blond hair. Though she was attractive, there was a manner about her that held back warmth.

Sarah was among the first to greet her, then said to Ross, "Where's Melissa?"

"My wife is meeting with a publisher in New York about the cookbook she's proposing," Ross said proudly. He turned to Cooper. "Thanks to you, Coop, for helping her find the right publishing house for her idea."

Cooper gave him a look of appreciation. "I can't wait to try some of those recipes. They all sound fabulous."

"And easy," said Ross. "Melissa hopes that will be the appeal of the book."

Poppy Browning, owner of the Wild Flower Boutique, arrived with a dentist in town, Dirk McArthur, and his wife, Samantha.

"Guess it's a full house," said Dani. "My sisters and I hope you'll all come to our party on Saturday."

Aaron turned to Sarah. "Will you be able to make it?"

"Yes, my mother will take the girls overnight. They love

having a sleepover, and I won't have to worry about what time I get home."

"Nice to have her help," said Aaron. "When I come into the store, I see your office light on upstairs. I know how busy you are."

Sarah chuckled. "My parents know exactly when I arrive and when I leave."

Aaron gave her a steady look. "Are you happy here? At one time, you couldn't wait to leave Lilac Lake."

She sighed and looked away. "That seems a lifetime ago. I had to leave, go to college as my parents hoped for me."

"Everything in its time. I had to stay in town and help Brad with the business we created in high school," said Aaron.

"And now you're so successful," said Sarah. "I'm proud of both of you. The Meadows is a stunning development."

"Thanks," said Aaron. "I've kept a large, wooded lot for myself."

From across the table, Tessa gazed at Aaron. "You're one of the developers for The Meadows? The houses there are gorgeous. A little pricey for me, but maybe someday."

"Are you planning to stay in Lilac Lake for some time?" Hazel asked.

"Under the right circumstances, I'd like to," said Tessa. "I'm single and hope to meet lots of people. At my interview, Ross told me that there's an active community of young people." Her gaze turned again to Aaron.

Aaron was facing Hazel, and now he was asking her how her teaching job was going.

Damon left his job behind the bar and walked over to the group. "Mind if I join you?" He took a seat. "How's everyone doing? Do you have any suggestions for the new menu?

JayJay and I want to change things up a bit."

"As long as you keep your chicken Caesar salad on the menu, I'm fine," said Whitney.

"Yeah, and the blue cheese burgers," said Nick, laughing as Whitney rolled her eyes at him.

"In the winter months, you'll want to have a nice soup," said Dani.

"And chili," said Brad. "We working guys need something substantial."

"Okay." Damon turned to Tessa. "How about you? Any suggestions?"

"Apple pie," Tessa said. "A tasty fall and winter dessert."

Ross introduced Tessa to Damon, and they exchanged smiles.

Hazel shot Sarah a glance and let out a soft sigh.

Sarah gave Hazel a look of encouragement. She knew when the time was right, Hazel would find the perfect man for her.

Shortly after Sarah finished her salad, she stood. "I'm sorry, but I have to get back home. Misty is watching the girls for me, and I don't want to be too late."

Aaron stood. "I'll walk you home."

"I'm going to stay for a while longer," said Hazel. She gave Sarah a little wink.

Flustered, Sarah said, "Are you sure you don't want to join us?"

"No, thanks. I'm not ready to go home."

Sarah waved to the group. "See you all on Saturday."

Aaron followed Sarah out of the restaurant and took her

elbow. "Glad you could have this time off. I meant what I said about wanting to take the girls apple picking."

She wondered if he was lonely. Growing up, he'd always been a bit of a loner but had never been without friends.

"I know you've had a hard time in the past few years, but I'm hoping we can renew our friendship," he said quietly, keeping pace beside her.

She stopped and gazed at him. "I'd like that very much. But, Aaron, I don't want you to get too close to me. I'm not who you think I am."

His warm gaze washed over her. "No matter who you think you are, I know what's inside you. That's all that matters to me."

Sarah turned away from him, feeling unworthy of his kindness. If he'd ever seen how frustrated, how unsympathetic she'd sometimes been to her husband's constant wars with himself and sometimes with her, he'd never want to see her again.

Aaron placed a hand on her shoulder. "The past is the past, Sarah. It's time for a new beginning." He forced her to face him.

Seeing his caring expression, tears filled her eyes. He was much too good for her.

Though they didn't talk the rest of the way to her cabin, he held her hand. When they reached it, they faced one another.

"I'm not giving up on you," Aaron said quietly, kissing her on the cheek.

The front door of the cabin opened, and Misty stood there. "Ah, I'm glad you're back. The girls are just getting ready for bed."

Emily and Mia came up behind her and grinned. "Aaron! I see you!" cried Mia.

"Me, too," said Emily.

"Hello, girls," said Aaron sweetly. "Sweet dreams." He'd seen them enough times to have them call him by name. Mr. Collister was too formal. And Sarah thought the use of "uncle" was a little creepy.

"Thanks for walking me home," Sarah told him. "Perhaps, we'll see you on Sunday, weather permitting."

"I'll see you on Saturday regardless of the weather," he said.

"Yes, of course," she answered. "It should be a fun party."

"'Night," said Aaron, before trotting back the way they'd walked.

Sarah went inside the house and took hold of the girls' hands. "I'll be right back," she said to Misty. "We have a new woman in town."

Sarah kissed each girl and left their room to speak to Misty, who was waiting for her in the kitchen.

"A new girl in town? What's she like?" Misty asked.

Sarah described her and said, "Ross brought her to the group gathering at Jake's, so she could meet people her age. She seems nice, but there's an edge to her that I can't explain. She's here as a single looking for someone."

"In this group, people are always pairing up. It'll be interesting to see what happens," Misty said. "We need to add some more men to the group."

"Damon and JayJay are both single. That should help. And Brooks Beckman is available."

"And adorable," said Misty. "I thought he'd be perfect for Hazel, but that didn't work." She cleared her throat. "I don't want to pry or push, but I hope you and Aaron can finally get together. I know you and he were a couple in high school. Is there anything between you now?"

Sarah leaned against the kitchen counter and let out a long sigh. "He deserves better than me. I failed him once, and I don't want to do it again."

"Failed him? What do you mean?" asked Misty. "You went to college, and he stayed home to grow his business in Lilac Lake. That's not failing him."

"It didn't take me long to hook up with the man who wanted to marry me. I even left college to do so. I had to finish my business degree online. If I'd waited, so many bad things might not have happened."

"And the girls?" asked Misty gently.

"They're the bright spots in my life. They were then, too, though I sometimes wonder if I'd been able to focus on my husband more, things might've ended differently."

Misty gave her a round-eyed look. "Wow! You're taking on way more than you have to for everything that's happened. You don't want to go down that path."

"I can't ignore what might've been," Sarah said, responding to Misty in a defensive tone.

Misty hugged her. "Anytime you want to talk about it, I'm here. I've got to go. My day starts early."

"Thanks for watching the girls ... and everything," said Sarah. "See you Saturday."

"You bet. David and I'll be there."

After seeing Misty out, Sarah watched Misty walk away and thought how lucky she was to have a friend like her.

She closed and locked the door and went to the girls' bedroom to watch them sleep. Mia was spread across the bed like a tossed doll. Emily, always more contained, curled up under her blanket.

She left their bedroom and went back to the kitchen to fix a hot cup of tea, hoping it would help her sleep. But thoughts of her deceased husband kept whirling in her mind. It had taken her a while to learn that behind the handsome man who was a ton of fun at school, there lurked a very troubled person.

Sarah sat at the kitchen table thinking of the past ...

She'd been so excited to learn she was carrying twins. And then seeing them, so much alike to strangers, so distinct to her, her heart had filled with a maternal love that continued to grow. Even now, tears stung her eyes as she observed them.

While she was working in an accounting firm, the fun of being a carefree college student evaporated. Sarah, who'd always been upbeat, kept things running smoothly at home until Jesse exploded with frustration one night and ended up weeping in despair. That was the moment she realized she couldn't ignore the fact that he needed outside help. By then, she was pregnant.

After the excitement of having twins had worn off and the real work of handling two infants day after day, night after night, Sarah and Jesse were too exhausted to cope with anything but survival.

Sarah's natural ability to overcome stress kicked in, but Jesse's depression grew worse. He started to drink, claiming Sarah wasn't giving him the attention he needed. And then he refused to take his medicine, saying it made him feel disconnected from his surroundings.

Sarah found a new doctor for Jesse, who told her that if Jesse didn't stop his destructive, addictive behavior, stronger actions might be needed.

When Jesse's behavior grew worse, Sarah tried to talk to him about it. But he had pushed her away, told her she was a terrible mother, a worse wife, and he wanted out of the marriage. The entire time he was crying.

Sarah tried to go to him, talk to him, but he stormed out of the house.

Later that night, still sick to her stomach from that dreadful scene, Sarah called a neighbor to watch the twins and went looking for him. That's when she discovered Jesse had shot himself in the head in the woods outside of town. At the same park where he'd proposed to her.

Now, although part of her recognized what people had told her about being a kind person who had tried to help, Sarah thought of herself as a failure.

It had been two and a half years since Jesse's suicide, and only one year since she'd been back home. In those in-between months, she'd been working on herself, getting counseling and dealing with the stress of living back home, right where she'd started.

CHAPTER THREE

SATURDAY EVENING, SARAH CLOSED AND LOCKED THE store's door behind her, ready for an evening of fun. Saturdays were the busiest days of the week because every "do-it-yourselfer" needed supplies and usually helpful advice. But tonight, she'd brush off any fatigue and enjoy the friends she had in town.

As Sarah walked home, she took her time, trying to decide what to wear to the party. It would be cool, and dress would be casual on this autumn evening. She wanted to look her best, be part of the more carefree group members.

The girls were already staying at her mother's house for the evening and overnight. With plenty of time to prepare, Sarah decided to soak in the tub. She'd washed her hair this morning and would need to do little else to get ready.

She drew the bath and had just lowered herself into the warm, scented water when her cell rang. *Hazel.*

Sarah reached for the phone sitting on the nearby counter. "Hello?"

"Hi, Sarah. It's me, Hazel. Do you want a ride to the party? I'd be happy to drive."

"Sure. That would be nice. Thanks."

"I think you ought to know that when Aaron returned to Jake's the other night, Tessa all but draped herself over him. She asked him to show her around town this weekend, and he said he would."

Sarah swallowed hard. "That was nice of him." She and Aaron had agreed to be friends, nothing more.

"I'm trying not to be quick to judge, but honestly, there's something desperate about Tessa that is uncomfortable."

"I don't want to get caught up in any negativity," said Sarah. "As you can imagine, I try to avoid that."

"I understand," said Hazel. "That's why I wanted you to know about it so you wouldn't be caught off guard."

"I appreciate that," Sarah said honestly. "But Aaron and I are just friends. So, I should be glad for him if Tessa is making her interest obvious, shouldn't I?"

"Theoretically, yes. But I'm not sure that's the real situation between you two. But I won't get involved except to make sure you know what's going on."

"Yes, it's best that way," Sarah said, feeling her stomach knot.

They ended the call, and when Sarah slid back into the water, she hugged herself, knowing she hadn't told the truth to Hazel. She wanted much more with Aaron, but she didn't see it happening. He deserved someone better than her. But she had the nagging concern that Tessa wasn't that person.

When Hazel picked her up for the party, she inspected Sarah's appearance and gave her a thumbs-up signal. "You look terrific. Are those leather pants new?"

"Yes, I got them at the Wild Flower Boutique. Poppy helped me pick them out. The brown leather and boots go well together, and I love the burnt orange sweater she sold me. Very fall-like."

"Very stunning," said Hazel. "Tessa is no match for you."

"Thanks, but I don't want to compete with her or anyone else. I'm pretty fragile."

Hazel gave her a quick hug. "I'm sorry. I don't mean to push you. I just see the way Aaron looks at you and ... "

Sarah held up her hand to stop her. "Thanks, but please stop."

"Okay, I promise," Hazel said, starting the car.

They were quiet on the way to the party, which suited Sarah. Like any small town, people got involved with other people's business. Hazel had meant only to be helpful, but Sarah realized she wasn't ready to move forward, not when she had so many doubts.

They arrived at Lilac Lake Cottage to find the porch and lawn filled with guests. Music played from speakers placed on the porch, almost overcome by the sound of laughter and conversation. It had been several weeks since Labor Day Weekend, and the group was ready to party.

"Let's join the fun," said Hazel, her eyes sparkling with anticipation.

Sarah grinned. "I'm ready to unwind."

They moved through the crowd to the bar set up on the porch. Sarah was careful how much she drank because of the girls, but she eagerly accepted a cup of beer poured from a keg. At times like this, she knew she'd made the right decision to return to Lilac Lake. Friends from years ago and new friends created an interesting support group.

Sarah gazed out over the crowd. She was glad to see Ross and Melissa. She'd thought Tessa had seemed a little too cozy with him Thursday night. She found Tessa in the crowd talking to Gage Martens, the handsome young veterinarian in town. On a whim, she decided to talk to him about an eventual dog for the girls. They loved Aaron's two black labs.

Gage gave her a big smile when she approached.

"I hope I'm not interrupting anything," said Sarah. "But, Gage, I wanted to talk to you about a dog for the girls in the future. They've started asking about one, and though I think it's too early for one, I want to do some research and need to get your opinion about a suitable breed for our situation."

"I'll see you later," Tessa said to Gage, and he looked relieved.

"Should I talk to you later? I don't want to interfere," said Sarah.

"Not at all. I was beginning to feel as if I was filling out an online dating form," said Gage. "I recently broke up with someone. I'm not ready to date for a while."

"I just met Tessa, so I don't know her well," Sarah said.

"She seems nice enough, just a little too desperate," said Gage. "Now, are you thinking of one dog or two for the girls?"

Sarah chuckled. "Definitely just one. And maybe something small and fun."

"I'll keep an eye out for you," said Gage. "Maybe a rescue that's already house broken?"

"That sounds perfect. I'm not in any hurry. But I don't want to say no forever."

Gage smiled at her. "I get it and appreciate your wanting to have things right before taking in a pet. Are you totally settled back in town? Like you, I've been here for only a year, but I really appreciate how supportive everyone is."

"As a teenager, I was eager to leave town. However, after

living away, I am truly glad to be back, even if my parents sometimes treat me like one."

Gage laughed. "Can I get you another beer?"

Sarah shook her head. "Not yet. Thanks."

Gage walked away, and Hazel approached her. "What did Gage have to say? I saw Tessa talking to him earlier."

"If you're interested in Gage, don't appear to be desperate. He told me that talking to Tessa made him feel as if he was completing an online dating questionnaire."

"I am interested in knowing more about him. He doesn't come to Jake's very often, and I haven't had much of a chance to spend time talking to him." She grinned. "Maybe I need a dog or a cat."

"Or a horse or a cow," Sarah teased.

"See you later," said Hazel.

Sarah was standing, looking around, when she felt Aaron's presence behind her. She turned and stared into those dark eyes of his, and a smile spread across her face.

"When did you get here?"

"A few minutes ago," he answered. "Your cup is empty. Can I get you more?"

"Sure. Why not? I'll be down at the rock," she said, walking away from him.

The cottage, now a lovely house, sat atop a small hill, whose slope led to the lake and an enormous rock that sat at the edge of the water. As kids, they'd all used the rock for sunbathing or reading or playing games. Even during fun parties like this, Sarah liked to escape for a few minutes of private time. The sound of the water lapping the shore and the light from the moon on the waves gave her an inner peace she knew she'd never be able to replicate anywhere else.

She was sitting on the rock, facing the water, when she felt Aaron's silent approach. She turned as he handed her the drink.

"It feels right to be here," said Aaron quietly as he sat beside her. "One of the things I've always admired about you is your ability to sit still and be quiet. How else can someone be aware of all that's going on in nature around them?"

"Is that something you learned from your mother?" Sarah asked.

"That, and so many things from the Abenaki Indian tribe," said Aaron. "I was lucky when my mother brought me to the Collister's home when she learned she was dying, but I'm luckier still to have been raised by her and with her beliefs during my early years."

"Do you go back to your family often?" Sarah asked.

"Whenever I can. My cousins live up by the Canadian border, and we like to hunt there," Aaron said. "But my life is really here. I owe my father's family so much."

As Aaron continued to stare out at the dark water, he took her hand in his.

"I admire your mother so much for having the courage to bring you here," said Sarah.

"Mr. Collister never knew about me until then. But she understood what kind of man he was and how warmly he would receive me."

"You must miss her terribly," said Sarah.

Aaron nodded. "But she speaks to me in the wind, and I know she is near."

Tears sprang to Sarah's eyes. Hearing such sweet, powerful words brought back the horror of the past couple of years. She realized that she and Jesse had never had the deep connection she had with Aaron.

Aaron got to his feet and extended his hand to her. "Let's join the party." She took hold of his fingers and allowed him to pull her up, facing him. They stared at one another for a moment, and then Aaron turned away. But not before she saw desire in his eyes.

Sarah followed him off the rock and up the hill to the rest of the party.

Aaron left her talking to Whitney. Because of her husband's job as police chief, Whitney was well-informed about what was happening in town. But she was discreet about not spreading information.

"I'm getting a little worried about handling a new baby with a toddler. How do you do it with twins? You always seem so calm."

"It can be difficult tracking the girls, who may be going in two different directions," Sarah admitted. "It's exhausting. It's one strong reason for my returning to Lilac Lake."

"Are you and Aaron seeing one another?" asked Whitney.

"We're friends. But that's all we've promised one another," Sarah said, realizing how sad that sounded.

"He's always been one of my favorite people," said Whitney, watching as he stood talking with a group of men. "Sexy, too."

Sarah felt her cheeks flush but said nothing. He was even sexier now than he'd been in high school.

Dani joined them. "It's turning into a wonderful party. Everyone seems to be having fun. I'm glad to see you here, Sarah. I know you can't always get out."

"Thanks. It's great to be here." She watched from a distance as Tessa approached Aaron.

"Tessa seems nice but a little overzealous about meeting new men," commented Dani. "I hope she doesn't make a mess of things."

As she spoke, Aaron gazed over to them with an unhappy expression.

"Oh, I'd better go rescue Aaron," said Dani. "As hostess, I don't want any of my guests to suffer." She winked at Sarah and hurried away.

Sarah went to talk to Melissa about her cookbook.

Melissa greeted Sarah with a warm hug. "How are you?"

"Good," said Sarah. "Ross proudly told the group at Jake's about your new cookbook. How's that going?"

"It's a lot harder than one would think," said Melissa. "I have to make sure all the recipes are tested for appearance, taste, and accuracy of measurements. Some of the recipes are from my work at Fins, but since the fire destroyed my parents' restaurant, I need to arrange a place to test the others."

"So, it'll be a while before it's ready?"

"Yes," said Melissa. "The fancy dinners Crystal and I had planned to put on every month or so will be a perfect place to start."

"You don't miss working at the restaurant?" Sarah asked.

Melissa shook her head. "No, especially now that I'm married to Ross. I need to have the flexibility to travel with him."

Taylor joined them and soon they were talking about her new book. After a while, Sarah slipped away.

Aaron came over to her. "Are we still on for apple picking tomorrow? Can I pick up you and the girls around ten?"

Feeling grounded once more, Sarah said, "That would be lovely."

CHAPTER FOUR

SARAH AROSE TO A BRIGHT, CRISP OCTOBER DAY, AND THE sound of her two daughters squabbling over a doll's dress. Turning her frown into a smile, Sarah got out of bed to see how she could help settle the feud. She'd picked them up from her mother's late last night so they could have a peaceful morning together before going apple picking with Aaron.

Mia and Emily loved one another dearly, but following the other's instructions didn't always happen. It was helpful that they were both independent and strong-minded, but it was exhausting to see this struggle being played out day after day.

She walked into the girls' bedroom. "Good morning! Let's have a nice day. What would you girls like for breakfast? After that, I have a treat for you. We're going apple picking with Aaron."

"Yay!" cried Mia and Emily together in a little chorus of joy.

"Let's put down the dolls and head to the kitchen for breakfast. Emily, it's your turn to choose."

"I want waffles," said Emily.

"Okay," said Sarah. "And we'll put fresh fruit on the side." She liked to balance treats with something healthier.

The girls chattered as they climbed up into their seats at the kitchen table.

"I like Aaron," said Emily matter-of-factly.

"And his dogs," added Mia. "How many apples can we pick?"

"We'll see," said Sarah, popping frozen waffles into the toaster. Sundays were days for lazy breakfasts.

"We're going to get a lot of apples today," said Mia.

"Lots of them," agreed Emily.

Sarah was grateful the girls were excited about their plans. Even if cooking all the apples in varying ways became a chore, picking apples was fun for all of them. She could already envision frozen apple pies, applesauce, and apple butter.

The girls were waiting, faces pressed up against the front window when Aaron pulled his silver truck into the driveway. The girls jumped off the couch and ran to the front door waiting like excited puppies as he got out of his truck and walked toward them.

"Hi, there," Aaron said, patting the girls on the back as they rushed forward and clutched his legs with excitement. "Are we ready for adventure? The sun is shining on us, a good sign."

"We want apples," said Emily.

"Lots of them," added Mia.

Chuckling, Aaron looked at Sarah. "Their enthusiasm is contagious."

Sarah laughed. "I've had to deal with it all morning. But I have the girls ready. We just need to grab a few things. I have a small cooler with water, along with some pretzels, and sunscreen, of course."

"After we pick apples, I'll treat you all to lunch," said Aaron.

He and Sarah loaded their things into the truck and worked together to install the safety booster seats Sarah had taken out of her car.

Aaron was a patient man, but Sarah could see he was finally ready to take off.

They drove to a well-known orchard outside of Londonderry. It delighted Sarah that her daughters were now visiting one of her favorite places from her childhood.

The Orchard, as it was called, contained trees holding three different kinds of apples and some pear trees. At Halloween, people could come to pick out pumpkins.

Aaron pulled into a parking space, and while he got out of the car with the cooler, Sarah spread sunscreen on the girls' faces and arms. They wore long pants and sturdy sneakers as the website suggested. Cute, pink, Red Sox baseball caps sat atop their blond heads.

Sarah whipped out her phone and snapped a few pictures just as an older couple walking by stopped. "Are they twins? They look exactly alike. So adorable."

"Yes," said Sarah. "Thank you. Come, girls."

They joined Aaron inside the main building, where he handed them plastic U-pick bags that the orchard provided.

"Ready? Let's go. I thought we'd start with the Cortland apples," said Aaron. "That's the closest station. Then, later, we can go to the Macoun apple station."

"Sounds perfect," said Sarah, satisfied he'd thought things through.

They headed out.

Sarah and Aaron walked together, pulling a wagon with

their cooler while the girls skipped and ran ahead of them.

The plan for The Orchard was well thought out and carefully developed after the original site was established in the late 1700s. Even with all the added tourist attractions, The Orchard buzzed with insects and came alive with the cries of birds.

"Ah, nature at its best," sighed Sarah.

"The Great Spirit has blessed this land," said Aaron. "Look at all this harvest."

Sarah smiled at him. "I love how you make life seem so spiritual."

He lifted her hand and gave it a squeeze. "Time to get the old Sarah back. I know you've been through a very difficult time, but you're still the person I once knew."

"Aaron, you deserve a woman who is whole," Sarah said, gazing at him with tenderness.

"I know what I know," said Aaron. "And our time will come."

Sarah was both thrilled and worried by his words. She'd meant what she'd said. He deserved better than her.

"I like this tree," said Emily, standing by a tree laden with delicious-looking apples.

"Okay, choose carefully and place the apples in the bag Aaron gave you," Sarah said. She was relieved the apple trees had been pruned earlier to allow many of the apples to be within easy reach.

Watching her children pluck apples from the tree, their faces alight with joy, Sarah experienced a pang of sadness that their father hadn't experienced moments like this.

After they picked enough Cortland apples, Sarah loaded their bags into the wagon and handed each of the girls another

U-pick bag. "These are for more apples. Let's go."

"I'm hot," said Mia, wiping her forehead.

Sarah handed each of the girls and Aaron a container of cold water. "Here you go."

"Ahh," said Aaron. "We must give thanks for water."

"Nice thought," said Sarah. "Can I hear a thank you from you girls?"

"Thanks," Mia and Emily said, and studied Aaron, who was tapping a hand to his chest over his heart as he looked up at the sky.

"Okay, on to the next spot," Sarah said, and the girls eagerly ran ahead of them as they walked to the Macoun apple section.

"You're talking more about your beliefs," she said to Aaron. "You didn't speak about them much in high school."

"No, I was trying to transition into my life in Lilac Lake. But it's important for me to return to my tribe every so often. It keeps me grounded."

As they drew closer, Sarah could see the girls reaching into the tree for apples.

Mia cried out and then burst into tears.

Sarah ran to her. "What's wrong?"

"Looks like a bee sting," said Aaron, taking hold of Mia's arm. "Hand me some of the water," he said to Sarah. He looked at the site of the sting and carefully rubbed a fingernail across it to pull out the stinger.

Emily stood by as Sarah held Mia, and Aaron poured some water on the dirt, mixing it into a paste. He took hold of Mia's arm and spread the mixture across the swelling. "I think I got the stinger. This should help take the soreness away until we get back to the main building. There, we can use soap and water for the wound and get some lotion for it."

Sarah looked at Mia. "Do you want to go back home, or do you want to stay and pick more apples?"

"I want to stay," said Mia. She held out her arm for everyone to see.

"Okay, then, we can pick more apples, but check to make sure it's in a spot that hasn't attracted a lot of bees," said Sarah.

"Bees usually don't sting unless in self-defense," said Aaron. "Just give them their space."

The girls stayed close as they all began to pick enough apples to fill their bags.

"Okay, that's enough," said Sarah laughing as she piled more full bags into the wagon.

"How about some ice cream?" Aaron said.

"Yay," said Emily. "I want strawberry."

"I'm going to have something else," said Mia.

They walked back to the main building which held an ice cream store and a farmer's market that sold fresh fruit and vegetables and farm items, including Aaron's maple syrup.

"First thing, Mia, is to get your arm cleaned up. How's it feeling?"

"Better," said Mia. "Hurry. I want my ice cream."

Sarah took both girls to the ladies' room and was washing Mia's arm when she heard Aaron call to her from outside the door. "I've got the first-aid cream."

"Go get it, Emily," said Sarah.

Emily returned with the cream, and Sarah gratefully spread it over the bite which was just a red mark on Mia's arm.

A few minutes later, the four of them were sitting at a table in the ice cream shop eating the most delicious vanilla fudge ice cream Sarah had ever tasted.

"At home, we can have an early dinner," said Sarah, wiping strawberry ice cream off Emily's face. "And Aaron, you're invited. I have a nice, easy way to cook chicken, and I make a mean salad."

Aaron licked ice cream from his cone. "That sounds delicious. While you were working on Mia's arm, I paid for the apples. They're in bags already loaded in the truck."

"Thanks," Sarah said, realizing how nice it was to have someone else helping her. Maybe, if Jesse had lived, a day like today might have happened. Maybe not.

At home, the girls were more than ready to sit in front of the television where they quickly fell asleep on the couch.

As Sarah organized the apples and prepared a number of them for the slow cooker recipe she had for applesauce, she and Aaron talked quietly about his work at the development. She spoke about her job at the hardware store as she fixed a chicken casserole.

"We've hired someone new," said Sarah. "A high school girl named April Loomis. She's gone through tutorial programs for dyslexia, and though letters are a problem, she's excellent with numbers. Her tutor is hoping that having a part-time job will help not only with finances, but will boost April's self-confidence."

"A good deed. I like it," said Aaron, smiling at her.

"We've hired her to help mark inventory. It's going to take extra time to teach her everything, but I'm hoping it will be worth it for both of us. My parents have always tried to help others. That's why our staff is so loyal to us. At one time or another they've all received some sort of extra help."

"I get it. Hazel has asked me to come to school and talk to her students about some of the stories from my tribe," said Aaron. "I figure it'll be interesting to them and helpful to my tribe for young people to learn about the people who were here before settlers arrived."

"Definitely," Sarah said. "You can talk to them about nature and your maple sugar trees, too"

"I save that talk for springtime." He studied her and then came closer. "Do you remember our high school years as much as I do?" he asked quietly.

Drawn into his dark-eyed gaze, she held her breath as he leaned forward and kissed her on the lips.

She closed her eyes and leaned into him, feeling for a moment that she'd been whisked back in time to when she was young and in love and free.

He wrapped his arms around her and hugged her to him.

She heard his sigh of contentment as she nestled against him. She felt the same way. He was her first love.

"Hey! What are you doing?" asked Emily, standing in the doorway staring at them.

Sarah jerked away from Aaron. "I'm just getting a hug. Want one too?"

Emily ran to her, and Sarah picked her up and gave her a growly bear hug, smiling at her daughter's laughter.

Mia appeared. "Me, too."

Sarah put Emily down and picked up Mia. When Sarah glanced at Aaron, he was smiling.

She had a flashback to the time when Jesse was alive and stood scowling at her when she was hugging the girls. It wasn't that Jesse was mean; he just had nothing to give them.

"How about a glass of wine while I get dinner ready?" she said to Aaron, putting Mia on her feet.

"Thanks. Do you need help?"

"Emily and Mia will set the table. If you'd like to pour the water and milk, that would be helpful."

She mixed a salad, adding slices of apples to the greens as a treat for the girls. She worked hard to make sure they ate balanced, healthy meals and weren't afraid to try something new.

After setting the table, Mia and Emily climbed into their booster seats and watched Aaron pour the drinks.

Sarah brought the salad and casserole to the table and allowed Aaron to help her get seated.

"Smells delicious," said Aaron, watching as she served the girls, then him.

After serving herself, Sarah looked at Mia. "It's your turn to say grace."

"Thank you for our food," said Mia. "And thank you, Aaron, for helping with my bee sting."

Sarah and Aaron exchanged smiles, and then everyone dug in.

They'd just finished their meal when Sarah's mother called.

Sarah let it go to voicemail. She didn't want anything to ruin this time with Aaron. Her mother hadn't thought Aaron was good enough for her in high school when he'd decided not to go to college. Now that Aaron was a successful owner of a business, he was deemed very suitable. Sarah wanted this time with Aaron to be private.

After dinner, the girls raced to their room to play.

While Sarah was putting dishes in the sink, Aaron came

up behind and gave her a hug. “Thanks for a special time. I’d better leave. It’s a busy day tomorrow, and I’ve got dogs waiting for me at home.”

She turned around and faced him. “It’s been a fun-filled time together. It means a lot to me that you enjoy the girls.”

“And you,” he said, his dark eyes twinkling. He straightened and grew serious. “Let me know when we can do something together again. I’ll try to make it to Jake’s next Thursday.”

“I will too,” said Sarah, purposely avoiding saying more. She couldn’t push a relationship between them when she knew from her past how everything could change and become something horrible. That’s how it had been with her and Jesse.

CHAPTER FIVE

ON MONDAY AFTERNOON, SARAH WAITED IN HER OFFICE to meet April Loomis, the high school girl who was starting her part-time job with them. She'd spoken with her tutor, Mary Alice Toomey, and they'd decided it was important for April to arrive by herself.

Sarah and Mary Alice had already discussed aspects of April's dyslexia and how capable she was with numbers.

"She's a lovely girl but needs help with her self-esteem. Needless to say, she's been bullied by others in school," said Mary Alice. "She lives with her father and grandmother, neither of whom is helpful when it comes to styles and such. I think spending time with you will be helpful in many ways. You might even be able to guide her toward a better appearance."

"I'll try," said Sarah. "Appearance does matter. Especially in high school, which is a tough place for many at best."

"I'm sure your parents are delighted to have you back in town. And I hear your daughters are adorable."

"Thanks. They're a handful but a lot of fun," said Sarah. "I'll get back to you in a day or two, after I've had a chance to see how April will fit in."

"Thanks. And if you need me at any time, just phone or text me. I appreciate your help," said Mary Alice.

Sarah ended the call and sat a moment. Being a part of

the summer gang had helped her through high school. That, and the fact that she was easy-going and liked to have fun. It made it easy to be included in the group of fun kids. She sometimes wondered what had happened to that lucky girl. One thing was for sure, if April needed her help, she would be glad to do so.

April arrived right on time at two thirty.

Sarah's gaze took in a girl of average height and size, brown hair, and pretty blue eyes. She was wearing a blue skirt, a white blouse, and white sneakers.

"Hi, April," said Sarah, getting to her feet. "We're glad you've agreed to help us out for a while. I think you'll like the job. Unloading stock, opening boxes is a little like Christmas."

April lips stretched into a nervous smile. "Thanks for having me. Ms. Toomey told me I was lucky to get this job, but that I was excellent with numbers, and that's what you needed."

"Exactly," said Sarah. "I also know how careful you are about doing your work and completing it. That means the world to us."

April stood quietly, clinging to her hands.

"This downstairs floor is where most of the receivables are entered into our computer system, marked, and stored. From here it goes into our display of goods. The heavier, bulky items like mowers and snow blowers are brought to a storage area near our receiving dock to be entered in our system and marked."

"Are all the holiday things stored here? I thought I saw a Christmas tree," said April gazing around the large space.

"Yes. We can have some fun with some of the Halloween things I've ordered. I'm going to do a holiday window display, and our store will be a stop on the Halloween parade of treats."

"Nice," said April. "The kids in my neighborhood love to get dressed up. I'm too old."

"If you want to be part of handing out candy here for the parade, you can dress up then," said Sarah. "We could use the help."

"Okay," said April, her eyes shining.

At that moment, Sarah knew she'd do anything to help April. She'd already seen beneath her solemn, anxious appearance to the adorable, eager girl just waiting to bloom.

Sarah led April over to a long table where a small box sat. A larger box sat on the floor.

"This is where we receive orders. We open the box, get the packing slip out, and check to make sure everything that is on that sheet is actually here in the box exactly as ordered. Sometimes descriptions are available. Other times, only the numbers for different items are shown."

April nodded politely.

Sarah held up the box cutter. "This is very sharp. You need to be careful with it and very careful opening the boxes, so you don't harm yourself or what's inside the box. Here."

April accepted the cutter from Sarah and worked carefully to open the box.

"These are for my Halloween display," said Sarah. "A black cat, a witch's hat, and some little stuffed mice. Look. Each mouse is a little different. This is where you have to be careful in checking them off on the packing slip."

Sarah let April set the pace as she worked her way

through the items in the box.

When she was done, Sarah said, "Okay, now we have to enter these items into the computer. First, we look for the company and bring up its account in our system. Then we enter the date we received it, today, and then we use our automatic screening device to input the numbers to our computer. In doing so, it will automatically determine the sales price. When that work is completed, we can print off a sheet of sticker prices to use for each item."

April studied the sheets.

"So, it makes sense?"

April gave her an unsure look. "Yes, but I'll need to do it a few times to get comfortable."

"Of course," said Sarah. "That's how we all learn. Let's complete this exercise by tagging only what items we are going to sell. We can keep the others without tags because they're part of our window decorations and can't be sold."

Sarah stood by, reminding herself not to jump in as April figured out which of the items needed tagging. She wanted to give April a chance to have some success.

"There," said April. "I'm done."

"Great," said Sarah. "Now I need to show you how you put tags on soft items like these. Other items in other boxes may need stickers affixed to them."

Later, after stowing the display items on a special shelf, Sarah turned to April. "Okay, we're done for the day. Do you have a way to get home?"

"I brought my bike," said April.

"Are you able to come after school tomorrow?" At April's nod, Sarah continued. "Let me show you the clock where you check in and out. It's important you do it both times so we can get your hours for payroll. Don't worry. I'll make a note on the card that you arrived at two thirty."

"Thank you," said April. "I liked doing this work. It was fun."

"I'm glad because we're going to need your help. Fall and the holidays are busy times for us."

They went to the check-in area in the receiving dock.

After she checked out, April's gaze remained on Sarah even as she spoke shyly. "Thank you very much."

"See you tomorrow," said Sarah, seeing April off and then going to check on her father, who was handling the cash register. "I'm going home. Anything else you need?"

He shook his head. "No, you go ahead to those girls. I'll take care of the late crowd and then close up."

Sighing with relief, Sarah headed back to her desk to gather her things.

On the way to pick up the twins, Sarah wondered how she should approach April's appearance. Working behind the scenes, opening boxes, and moving things around, a skirt and blouse were not appropriate choices for her. In addition, they made April look as if she was wearing someone's cast off clothing. A cause for bullying.

She felt maternal juices flowing through her just thinking of it. She'd have April wear one of the store's blue polo shirts and tell her to wear jeans. That would be practical and give her an updated look.

On the spur of the moment, she decided to drop the polo shirt off at April's house. She lived in a neighborhood not too far from the cabin complex where Sarah lived. She'd go there first and then pick up Mia and Emily.

She got a shirt, wrapped it in tissue, and stuffed it into her purse. She didn't want to overstep any boundaries with April's family, but she couldn't bear the thought of April being teased. The young girl was so eager to please, so smart with numbers.

As she left the store, she felt satisfied about the day. Hopefully, the rest of the week would prove to be as pleasant.

When she approached the small house, she noticed the leaves in the yard, the need for paint on the old gray clapboards. Sarah knew that April lived with her father and grandmother but had very little knowledge about either of them.

She knocked on the front door.

It was opened by a woman with gray, almost white hair, wearing a long black dress.

Startled, Sarah said, "I hope I have the right address. I'm looking for April Loomis."

"Wait just a minute." The older woman left her standing on the porch, but Sarah could hear her call April's name inside.

April came running to the door, her cheeks flushed. "Hi, Sarah. Is something wrong?"

"No, I just wanted to tell you that you did an excellent job today, and as a new staff member, you get to wear one of our shirts with your jeans to work. It's a uniform of sorts."

Sarah handed the tissue-wrapped package to April, who took it eagerly and opened it.

"I love it!" she cried, holding it to her chest. "I'll wear it tomorrow."

"What's this?" asked the older woman.

April turned to her. "It's my new uniform for work, Grandma. A shirt that I'll wear with jeans."

Her grandmother studied it. "I guess it's okay. It's not one of those shirts that show a girl's belly. And no tight jeans and makeup for you."

April rolled her eyes. "I wouldn't wear them anyway. Sarah, this is my grandmother Priscilla Loomis."

"It's nice to meet you." Sarah held out her hand and after some confusion, Priscilla shook it.

"Thank you for stopping by," said April. "See you tomorrow."

Sarah hesitated then decided to ask, "Where's your father? I was hoping to tell him what a helpful job you'll be doing for us."

"He's a long-distance truck driver and is away. That's why my grandmother lives with us."

"Oh, I see. Maybe later I'll have the chance to meet him." Sarah was aware April's grandmother was listening to everything being said.

She left the house unsettled. April might be more in need of the job than she'd first thought. It seemed as if she was being far too sheltered by a woman who'd not kept up with the times.

CHAPTER SIX

That night, Sarah sat and watched the girls play in the bathtub. They were best buddies and had developed rules between them as to who would be in charge from time to time, sharing that privilege.

While growing up, she'd longed for a sibling. That's why her friends in town were so important to her. It was unique for so many of the summer crowd to return to town and resume their old friendships. A lot of that had to do with Genie Wittner, the grandmother of the Gilford girls and the former owner of the Lilac Lake Inn, which had been in her family for generations. Even now, she was considered a matriarch by many of the townspeople.

What would have happened if, after college, she and Jesse had returned to Lilac Lake instead of going to South Carolina? Would the town have been able to support Jesse through his depression? Sarah had wanted more time away. But maybe that was another mistake of hers.

The girl's playing turned into squabbles.

"Okay, time to get out and into our PJs," said Sarah, holding onto one of the girls and then the other as they climbed out of the tub.

As she wiped each face dry, she kissed it. She'd always wanted to be a mother. And though having two at once had its challenges, Sarah would be open to more children if the right person came along.

Her thoughts immediately swerved to Aaron. He was such a kind man. The best she'd ever known. Which is why they'd remained special friends.

The next morning, after dropping the girls off at preschool, Sarah thought about the three weeks ahead before Halloween. By then, she hoped April would be comfortable enough to wear a costume and help with the event at the store.

As she walked along the sidewalk, she admired the leaves changing colors on the trees. Lilac Lake enjoyed a busy "leaf-peeper" season, with people coming from all over to view the stunning colors of autumn leaves in New England. Afterward, the town swung into Christmas festivals before welcoming the skiers, who came to ski on nearby mountains. It was this continuity that had helped her family grow the hardware store into a major retail business in the area.

In town, she observed Poppy Browning watering the potted, colorful fall flowers in front of her store, the Wild Flower Boutique. "Good morning!" she called to her.

"Hi, Sarah. I was going to call you today to tell you that the sweater you ordered just came in. You're going to love it."

"Thanks. I'll stop by later. I'm off to the café and then to work," said Sarah continuing on her way. It was this feeling of belonging that kept her going when she was having a difficult day.

At the café Crystal had run for years, she greeted the new owner, Nettie Mancini, and stood in line to order her usual coffee. Whitney appeared with her son in a stroller.

"Guess everyone needs a morning break," she said

pleasantly. "I hope you'll be at Jake's on Thursday. We're surprising Poppy for her birthday."

"Oh, yes. I'll be there. That's usually my weeknight out," Sarah said. "Can I bring anything?"

"No," Whitney said. "Crystal is baking a cake. That's it."

After getting her coffee, Sarah hurried across the street to open the store. It was her day to do so. She unlocked the main door and stepped inside. The store had a distinctive smell, not an unpleasant one, but one that indicated it was filled with all kinds of items from paint to cleaning supplies, to sweet gifts.

After snapping on the lights and switching the "Open" sign around, she climbed the stairs to her office. A print-out of yesterday's sales was waiting on the printer. She'd use that to help determine what needed to be ordered.

Downstairs, she heard the jingle of the door and looked down through her glass window to see Aaron standing there.

Sarah automatically swiped a hand through her hair and headed down the stairs.

"Hello," she said cheerfully.

"Hey, there. I need to pick up a few things and charge it to our account." Aaron gave her the shy smile that always tugged at her heartstrings.

"No problem. Pick out what you need, and I'll be glad to ring it up to your account. Need my help?"

"Did you get in a new supply of drywall nails? You were running low last time I was here."

"They came in yesterday," said Sarah, leading him to the aisle where they were sold. She reached up and withdrew a box of them from the shelf. Just as she turned to face him, she bumped into him reaching for a different box.

They stood a moment gazing at one another.

Sarah resisted the internal pull she felt to lean into him, and jumped back awkwardly, tripping on her own feet.

"I've got you," said Aaron, placing his strong fingers around her arm and pulling her toward him.

Feeling her cheeks heat, she lifted her gaze to meet his. It felt just like a kiss.

"Aw, I can't help it," said Aaron, wrapping his arms around her. "You're beautiful."

This time, Sarah nestled against him, hearing the racing of his heart. After a delicious moment of connection, she forced herself to pull away from him, overwhelmed by a memory of how she'd failed her husband.

"I know you've had some horrible things happen to you, but you can't allow them to ruin your life going forward. I can't believe the man you loved enough to marry would want you to do that. True?" Aaron's gaze bore into her, waiting for her answer.

Conflicted, Sarah frowned. "I'm not sure. Things got very bad toward the end. I thought I was helping ..."

"Yoohoo! I'm here!" came a cry.

At the sound of her mother's voice, Sarah stood straight, brushed off her shirt and answered. "I'm with a customer."

Aaron studied Sarah for a moment, then took the box from her and walked off with it and the box he'd taken from the shelf.

She heard her mother greet him and slipped up the back stairs to the second floor so she wouldn't have to speak to either one of them.

At her desk, she took a long sip of coffee and let out a sigh. She and Jesse had been in love when they married. Of course, they had. They were thought of as the perfect couple, so it seemed natural to marry even before Sarah had finished her degree.

Sarah realized it was important to remember how much they'd loved one another in the beginning. She'd never understood what had brought on his horrific periods of depression. It was almost as if his busy college life had hidden them.

She remembered how Jesse had hated his job after the excitement of getting it was gone. They'd talked about it and had even agreed that he needed to increase the dosage of his anti-anxiety medication.

After the excitement of the birth of the twins had worn off, Jesse began to obsess about her need to take care of them. And when Jesse and she were exhausted caring for the girls twenty four/seven, they began to attack one another. Jesse could be vicious about needing time alone, away from the family, and her. She'd cried foul and worse.

At the time, Sarah was unaware that her husband was trying other pills. Pills that undermined his strength by giving him the idea of committing suicide. By the time, he could no longer stand his mental anguish and decided to end it all, she'd discovered he'd been living a secret life of taking a mixture of drugs. She'd been furious with him before guilt took over, convincing her that, had he lived with a different woman, he might not have taken his life to escape the one he had with her.

Counseling had helped, but nothing would take away the pain, the sorrow, the blame from her. She tried her best to keep that hidden inside.

Now, the sound of her mother walking into the upstairs space jarred Sarah from her morbid thoughts. By the time her mother came into her office, Sarah had pulled herself together.

"It looks like another busy day," said Sarah's mother. "How did the new intern, April Loomis, work out yesterday? Do you need our other high school worker to help her?"

"April did just fine. I don't think it's a wise idea for Wyatt Wilson to be in on our sessions. Not yet. April is shy and vulnerable. Besides, we hired him to unload trucks and do some heavy work around the place. She'll be working for me."

"Okay. April is in your hands," said Sarah's mother. "I'm just thankful we can be of some benefit to both of them."

After her mother left her office, Sarah got to work, making a list of things to go over with April. She was excited to see how April looked when she arrived. She hoped wearing the shirt with the store logo on it would give her a feeling of belonging.

That afternoon, Sarah looked up from her desk to see April walking toward her wearing a skirt and a blouse. Surprised, she waited for April to speak.

"Hi," said April. "I need just a few minutes to change. My grandmother was upset that I was wearing jeans, so I told her I'd change. But I brought the jeans and the shirt with me, so I'd be in uniform." Her lips curved, sending a light to her beautiful green eyes. "She'll get used to the idea, but I'll go slowly."

After April left her, Sarah seethed inside at the notion that a high school girl wasn't allowed to wear jeans to school like the other kids in town, making her seem apart.

When April returned, she looked attractive in the

"uniform", or maybe it was the joyful look on her face that caught Sarah's attention.

"Okay, ready to work?" Sarah said, deciding not to get in the middle of a family squabble.

"Yes, I'm really excited about doing this," said April, taking a seat in the chair Sarah had pulled up to her desk.

"Yesterday, we put labels on items to sell and entered them into the computer program. Now, let's check to see if any sales were made with them," said Sarah. "You'll be doing the labeling, but I want you to see the results. Most times, it takes days for a sale to ring up on a new item. But because those were seasonal, we might have sold one or more overnight. Let's check."

Sarah showed April how to get into the program and go to the items they'd entered. Two of the items had sold – a mouse and a witch.

April's eyes widened at the sight of them. "That's really cool. Can we put in more inventory today?"

"Yes. I've saved a box for you to do. I'll sit with you, but I won't say a word unless you're about to make a wrong move. I've printed out the steps for you to follow. Let's go over them."

They moved to the receivables area where a box was waiting to be opened. After going through the routine on paper, Sarah had April begin.

Once April got past the first item, she was quick and accurate.

"You're doing a great job," said Sarah. "I'm leaving work early today. I'm going to get some highlights put into my hair. I need a haircut too."

April studied her. "I'd like to get my hair done like yours. I'll save up for it."

Sarah didn't encourage or discourage her. She'd heard how Misty got in trouble at school for trying to help a student. And she didn't want this situation to go bad.

Later, sitting in *Styles*, the hair salon owned by Gracie Milner, a pleasant woman in her fifties, Sarah felt herself relax. She didn't often fuss over herself, but a new hairdo and streaks of blond through her brown hair were exciting. She'd been feeling frumpy.

Having an appointment at *Styles* meant catching up on the news in town. But Gracie never allowed herself or her staff to talk mean about anyone. Her business was too important to her.

While she was waiting for her color to come up, Sarah sat to one side while Gracie trimmed the bangs of a little girl, Cecily, who went to preschool with Mia and Emily.

It was an unexpected opportunity to chat with the little girl's mother, a nice woman who was busy with a houseful of older boys.

"I just love being here. She's such a pleasure after my boys," gushed Cecily's mother. "Your girls are so adorable. We should try to get them together to play some weekend."

"Yes, that would be nice. Weekends are busy at the store, but maybe we can work something out," said Sarah. "I know how important it is for them to have friends."

When it was time for Sarah to get back into Gracie's chair, she sat and looked at herself in the mirror, grinning at the number of foils in her hair. It was time to add some fun to her looks.

Later, Sarah hugged Gracie. "Thanks so much. I love it."

Her brown hair streaked with blond met her shoulders in an easy bob. It was long enough to pull back if she needed to but hung nicely when she wanted to keep it flowing.

When she picked up the girls at preschool and heard them cry, "Pretty, Mommy!" she knew the effort had been worth it. More than that, through her visit to the salon, the girls had an opportunity to make a new friend.

CHAPTER SEVEN

The next day when April walked into Sarah's office, she was wearing her jeans and the polo shirt. She took one look at Sarah's new hairdo and clapped her hands. "That's what I want to do with my hair."

"No problems wearing the jeans and polo shirt today?" Out of her usual skirt and blouse, April's figure was both sleek and appealing. She'd also tied her hair back into a ponytail.

"My dad came home last night," said April. "He said I could wear them, no problem. My grandmother had become very strict and old-fashioned since my grandfather died. I'm going to ask Dad for some new clothes." She held a finger to her lips. "And I'm going to surprise him with a new hair style like yours."

Sarah was both touched by April's desire to change and concerned. She didn't want any problems with April's grandmother once her father left again. After the time spent training her, Sarah needed to know April would be able to work for them without any problems from home.

"Take it one step at a time," said Sarah. "We've got a big Christmas shipment in. Are you ready to get to work?"

They were busy unpacking the boxes and doing content checks when Wyatt Wilson appeared. He was the picture of a healthy, outdoor-looking guy with blond hair and blue eyes.

He looked startled to see April.

"Hi, Wyatt. Do you know April Loomis? April, this Wyatt Wilson. I believe he's a year ahead of you at the high school."

April's cheeks turned a pretty pink. She glanced at Wyatt. "Hi."

Wyatt gave her an appreciative look and turned to Sarah. "Your mother says I need to bring in some of the bigger boxes of stuff."

"Yes. It's those three boxes by the back door," Sarah said.

He gave her a salute, grabbed all three boxes in his strong arms and left them by April, giving her a last look before leaving.

"Wow!" said April a little breathlessly. "His girlfriend is one of the meanest girls at school."

"Really? He's a nice young man," Sarah said. "Hardworking."

April stared at the doorway where Wyatt had disappeared and then turned back to the sheet they'd been working on.

Sarah was interested to see that once April understood the process, she was careful to check her numbers. She had a feeling April wouldn't need help from her any longer, which was a good thing because overseeing inventory was just one of Sarah's jobs. Sarah didn't know that much about dyslexia but was determined to learn more. It was confusing that someone who had difficulty with letters could do so well with numbers. One thing was certain; April was a bright young woman.

April and Sarah left the store together. Instead of using her bike, April announced she was walking home. "I need the exercise," she explained.

"I like walking myself. How long have you been working

with Mary Alice Toomey as your tutor?" Sarah asked.

"For about two years. We've only been in Lilac Lake for that amount of time. My father came here to go fishing, saw Lilac Lake, and decided to rent a house here. He thought my grandmother and I might like it better than living in a town outside Boston."

April gave her a sad look. "My mom died a couple of years ago. That's when my grandmother came to help my father. He's a wonderful man who refuses to get caught up in a corporate lifestyle again. He says he likes being on the open road."

"Do you see him often?" Sarah asked, hoping she wasn't being too nosy.

"Pretty much. He tries to make it to important events in my life, and he likes to hunt and fish." Love shone in April's eyes, and Sarah wondered about the man who'd arrived in town a short while before she'd come back.

April stopped walking and faced Sarah. "I know my dad will give me the money I need for new clothes, but I don't know exactly what to get. Will you help?"

Sarah glanced at the doorway of The Wild Flower Boutique. "Yes, I will. But I know someone who can do an even better job of that. Let me introduce you to Poppy Browning. She owns this store."

April looked at the store wide-eyed. "But her things are so pricey."

"She knows a lot about fashion and what's in and out and how to make use of a few staple pieces. Trust me, it'll be like having your own personal shopper. Okay?"

A wide grin crossed April's pretty face. "Okay."

They entered the store and waited patiently for Poppy to

finish with a customer, who left the store carrying a large bag.

Poppy turned to them. "Hi, Sarah. How are you liking the sweater I ordered for you?"

"I love it," Sarah said. "I want to introduce you to April Loomis. She's my new intern at the store and is looking for a makeover of her clothes. Her budget is limited, but I knew you'd have a ton of ideas for her. Will you help?"

Poppy's warm brown eyes lit with pleasure. She held out her hand. "It's nice to meet you, April. You couldn't work for a better person than Sarah."

Sarah realized that the whole time Poppy was talking to April she was sizing her up for style and color. She was someone who knew exactly how to bring out the best appearance in another.

"Someone doesn't have to spend a lot of money to get the right look, the right style," said Poppy. "You just need to know quality and color. My favorite place to shop is T.J. Maxx. I bet we could find a lot for you there." Poppy patted her pink sweater. "Cashmere at a bargain price."

April looked as if she was about to twirl around the room with excitement.

"Of course, I'd need approval from your parents in order to do this," said Poppy. "But I'd love to help."

"My father is in town. I'll see if I can get him to come meet you," said April. "Thank you."

"Thanks," Sarah said. "I'll talk to you later." She knew that Poppy was sometimes lonely, and this would fill some hours and be a perfect way for her to help April.

The next morning, Sarah was working at her desk when

her father arrived with a man in tow.

"Sarah, this is April's father, Blake Loomis. He'd like to speak to you about April."

She stared in surprise at a tall, well-built man with dark hair that had turned gray at the temples. His steel-gray eyes studied her as he walked forward to greet her. He wore a pleasant smile that made it easy for Sarah to respond in kind.

They shook hands, and then Sarah said, "Please. Have a seat and tell me what I can do for you."

He lowered himself into a chair in front of the desk and studied her. "So, this is the woman who's been putting all kinds of ideas in my daughter's head."

Sarah stiffened. "I'm not sure what you mean."

"She's suddenly interested in clothes and is a different person talking about her job and the uniform you have her wear. I'm not sure what to think about it."

Sarah studied him, unsure how to answer. He didn't seem angry. Just curious. She decided to be open with him. "Between her tutor and getting this job here, I believe April is finally gaining self-confidence. I understand she's been bullied at school but is handling herself with more strength. She's a very bright girl."

"I know that. That's why we're here," said Blake matter-of-factly. "Someone told me about Mary Alice Toomey and the work she did for a child of his, and I decided to move to Lilac Lake for that reason. April thinks it's because I love to hunt and fish. While that's true, the real reason is my daughter's happiness."

"Very nice, because it's working," said Sarah.

"So, this clothing thing is important?" he asked.

"Very important," said Sarah. "April naturally doesn't

want to be teased for her clothes and overall appearance. She mentioned that her grandmother is old-fashioned."

"Yes, my mother is appalled by what she sees girls wearing today. While I won't allow April to go crazy with bad choices, my daughter should not be an outcast because she's forced to wear out-of-date clothes." He looked down at the T-shirt and jeans he was wearing. "I'm no fashionista, but there's nothing wrong with clothes like these."

"I agree. April is someone who's eager to please, and with you away, she didn't want to fight with her grandmother."

Blake looked down at the floor. When he lifted his face, Sarah could see sadness in his eyes. "After my wife's death, I decided to leave my corporate job and do something entirely different. Maybe I've been selfish, but I thought having my mother living with us would help us all. Now, I'm not so sure. We've all been a little lost."

Sarah's heart went out to him. "I lost my husband, which is why I moved back to town. You'll find people here are very kind. In fact, I want you to meet Poppy Browning, a friend of mine, who's willing to help April with smart shopping. A group of us in town likes to meet up at Jake's in the evening. Why don't you join us Thursday night anytime between 6 and 10? And if you'd like, I'll take you to Poppy's store so you can meet her."

"That would be nice of you," said Blake. "I'm ready anytime."

Sarah checked her watch. "April isn't scheduled to come into the store today. Let's go."

As they walked down the street to Poppy's store, Sarah

talked to Blake about some of the shops and people in town. "I really think it would be helpful for you to meet us at Jake's. It's a great group of people. You might even know of Ross Roberts."

"Ross Roberts, the baseball player?" Blake asked.

Sarah grinned. "He's part owner of the Lilac Lake Inn and is married to one of my friends. You'll like him."

"You sure know how to convince a guy," said Blake.

Sarah laughed. "Like I said, it's a good group.

As they approached The Wild Flower Boutique, Sarah wondered how Poppy would react to her bringing a very handsome man into her store and announcing that he was April's father.

Poppy was standing on a stool with a long-handled duster in her hand when we walked inside the shop.

"Hi, Poppy. I have someone I want you to meet. April's father."

When Poppy turned to stare down at us, the ladder wobbled.

Blake moved quickly to steady Poppy and held onto her as she climbed down awkwardly.

"Sorry about that," Blake said staring into Poppy's face.

Poppy's cheeks turned pink as she gazed at him.

Sarah waited a few seconds, enjoying the way they were looking at one another, and then cleared her throat. "Poppy, this gentleman is April's father, Blake Loomis. When I told him you were going to help his daughter, he wanted to meet you. Blake, this is Poppy Browning, owner of this store."

They shook hands and then Blake gazed around with confusion.

"I'm not proposing to help your daughter find bargains

here," said Poppy. "I've suggested finding clothing for her at discount prices. I love fashion for all ages and think I can help your daughter find suitable clothes and show her what to look for at the same time."

"Why would you do that?" he asked.

"Because I know what it's like to need some help," Poppy said kindly. "I don't have children of my own, but I do understand the need for kids to fit in. I was like her at one time."

Standing in black pants with a white sweater and wearing a colorful French scarf tossed casually around her neck, Poppy was the picture of an attractive professional woman.

Blake seemed to think so too as his gaze lingered on her and a smile played at his lips.

"Well, I'm sure you have a lot to talk about, logistics and all that," Sarah said. "Blake, if you have any questions about April's job, feel free to ask. Poppy, I've invited Blake to join our get together Thursday night. Make sure he comes."

"Okay," said Poppy, her cheeks now a bright red.

Outside the shop, I turned and looked at the two of them still facing one another, thanking my lucky stars that my intuition was right on this. They seemed very compatible. And they both needed something like this.

CHAPTER EIGHT

The next afternoon, April was smiling as she walked into Sarah's office. "What did you say to my Dad? He's all for my getting new clothes and an updated look. He even said I could cut my hair. I think I'll surprise him with frosted streaks."

"Your father came into the office to meet me, and then I took him to meet Poppy. It must have been Poppy who got him to agree to everything. He seems like a very nice man and a loving father."

Still smiling, April shook her head. "You both are amazing. Dad apologized to me for not paying attention. He even told my grandmother to trust me to choose wisely for myself."

"That's a heavy burden," Sarah told April. "It means you're going to have to really think about things because like your grandmother believes, some young girls don't." I felt about one hundred years old saying this to her, but the thought of my sweet little girls becoming teenagers hit home.

"What's this about my Dad meeting a group of people in town tonight?"

"A group of grownups my age and a little older meet at Jake's a couple of times a week. It's a relaxing way to see people and get the latest news about what's happening in town. I think your father will like it. Sounds like he's been pretty lonely."

April let out a sad sigh. "It's been hard having my mother gone. Her eyes welled with tears. She quickly brushed them away. "But it's always been my father who told me over and over again that I wasn't stupid. He explained about dyslexia so I could understand why my brain wasn't functioning like the average person's. Albert Einstein, Leonardo da Vinci and many others were dyslexic. Still, try to convince some of my classmates ..." her voice trailed off.

"You're proving how smart you are with this job," Sarah said, giving her an encouraging smile.

"I'm really lucky to be here," said April.

"Have you thought anymore about the Halloween party for kids here at the store? It'll be a time to dress up and have some fun with them."

"I'll talk to my Dad about it tonight."

"I could really use your help. Wyatt has already agreed to do it."

April's face lit up. "Okay, then. I'll see what I can do."

It occurred to Sarah that both father and daughter needed a proper introduction to life in Lilac Lake. Poppy was the perfect person to do it.

After work Sarah hurried home, grateful for her mother's help in getting the girls from preschool and taking them for a sleepover. At first Sarah had fought the idea of returning to Lilac Lake after such a personal tragedy. But now she was glad she had. Without the support of her family and friends, she'd be left with nothing but her guilt for a companion.

She took time for a bath before getting ready to go to

Jake's. Time alone was such a gift.

As soon as she dressed and fussed with hair and a touch of makeup, Sarah went outside to head to town. It was a short, easy walk and one she enjoyed when she was feeling ready for some fun.

Jake's was busy on this fall evening, and Sarah was excited to see her friends spread out at the two back-corner tables the group had claimed as their own.

She did a quick glance around the table and didn't see Aaron, Poppy, or Blake. But Whitney and Dani were there with their spouses, along with Ross Roberts and Melissa Hendrickson, and a few other regulars. Hazel and Misty, she knew, were coming later after parents' meetings at the school.

A birthday cake sat in the middle of one table and pink balloons were tied to a chair.

"Guess we're ready for Poppy's birthday. It looks perfect." She slid into a chair next to Whitney and turned to everyone with a bright look. "What is it about our Thursday gatherings that makes the rest of the work week seem dull?"

"It's a fabulous break for us all," said Dani. "Especially during the fall and winter months when we in the contracting business can't work in the dark."

A waitress came over to the table, and they ordered drinks and food.

Just as Sarah began to wonder if Aaron was going to show up, he appeared with Poppy and Blake.

"Hey, everyone," said Poppy, standing with the men. "Meet Blake Loomis. He's fairly new in town and has a daughter in high school. Please introduce yourselves."

Aaron took a seat next to Sarah and patted her back. "I'm glad you could make it."

"Believe me, I love these Thursday evenings. How are things with you?" Though she tried to sound as if they were talking as friends, her heart was pumping inside her chest with excitement at seeing him again.

"Happy birthday, Poppy!" cried Whitney. "Have a seat in the birthday chair. We'll cut the cake whenever you're ready."

Poppy clutched her hands together. "This is so sweet. Thank you for thinking of me."

"You're a very important part of this town," said Sarah, and others at the table quickly agreed.

Poppy and Blake took seats across the table from Sarah. Though she knew Poppy was interested in Blake, she realized he was still grieving his wife's death. Still, there was something nice in the way they interacted with one another.

Blake began talking to Ross about baseball and several other conversations came up around the table.

Sarah turned to Whitney. "How are things coming for the Halloween parade? It's a good thing you're in charge because everyone seems to want to be part of it. I'm getting the stop at the hardware store organized. It should be fun."

"It's going to be spectacular," said Whitney. "Like you said, everyone in town wants to participate in the festivities. The Lilac Lake Inn is offering special meals for guests, and they will hold fireworks at nine. And the community center is being used for teens for a haunted house."

"It sounds like you have everything covered," Sarah said. "We've been selling witch's hats like crazy."

Whitney chuckled. "It's going to be so much fun."

Tessa, sitting next to Blake across from Sarah and Aaron,

reached across the table and grabbed Aaron's hand for attention. "I heard you love being outdoors. So, do I. Maybe we could go canoeing on the lake sometime. If I pack a lunch, will you take me?"

Sarah could sense Aaron's hesitancy before he spoke. "We can think about it."

"I'll call you soon, and we can set it up. I know you're busy at The Meadows with all the houses you're building. But I'm sure we can make time for a little fun."

Sarah took a sip of wine and turned to Whitney, desperate to get a conversation going with her. She didn't want to react to Tessa's invitation to Aaron, didn't want him to see her sudden jealousy. After all, how many times had she backed away from his advances when she knew he wanted more than friendship.

Whitney, who'd overheard Tessa, gave Sarah an encouraging look and said quietly, "Tessa's new and has no idea who Aaron is besides a hot guy."

As if reassuring her, Aaron turned to Sarah. "Can I walk you home tonight?"

"Yes. It's a beautiful evening. And I have the night free."

He clasped her hand and gave it a squeeze.

Tessa stared at them and finally turned to Melissa sitting beside her.

As Sarah had mentioned to Blake, it was fun to catch up with everyone's activities. This group represented a lot of important working people in their small town.

After the birthday cake had been cut, a horrible song had been sung, things began to die down,

"Ready to go?" Aaron said to Sarah, He held out his hand and she took it, knowing he was eager to talk to her.

###

Outside in the clear, crisp air, Sarah was satisfied she'd worn her new, warm sweater. She looked up at the stars in the sky, twinkling with messages for those who wanted them, and drew in a long breath. Fall was such a gorgeous time of year in New England.

Aaron put his arm around her, and they began their walk through town.

"It's always so pretty," sighed Sarah. Main Street was decorated at night with small white lights in and around the store fronts, in the potted plants and flowers, and wrapped around the decorative light poles. She chuckled. "The girls think it's a real fairyland."

"How are they?" Aaron asked. "No more bee stings?"

Sarah beamed at him. "They're fine. Busy as ever."

They approached the empty bench sitting in front of Petals, the flower shop in town, and Aaron pulled her to a stop. "Let's sit a moment."

They lowered themselves onto the bench and Aaron turned to her. "Growing up with my mother, I learned to wait for the things I wanted. I was taught to wait until the apples turned ripe or until the wheat was ready to harvest. That's how I feel about us. I love you, Sarah, and I will wait until we can harvest our love together."

Sarah's eyes stung with tears. She fought to contain them.

He lifted her chin and kissed her.

Even as she relaxed in his arms, she felt a part of her hold back. She'd loved him as a young, naïve girl who'd jump at the chance to say she loved him back. As an adult woman who carried such awful memories and blame for them, she hesitated.

"What if I can't move on?" she finally asked, like a weakling

"The sun and the moon will continue to rise and set, giving you time. But don't ask me to wait too long. I'm a man who is lonely for you."

"You know how I feel about you," she said. "But ..."

"You need to let the past go," Aaron said gently.

Crying now, she said, "I was the first one who found Jesse in the woods at a park. I will never forget what he did to himself. Maybe because of me." She covered her mouth at the sudden queasiness she felt.

"His spirit was sick, unable to heal," said Aaron. "Don't wait until it's too late to harvest what we have together."

"I understand. And if you want to go canoeing with Tessa, I'm sure she'd like it."

Aaron gazed into her eyes and chuckled. "You're a bit jealous."

Sarah could feel her cheeks grow hot and looked away.

"C'mon, let's get going," said Aaron getting to his feet.

Sarah gazed up at him and knew in her heart he was right. They were meant to be together. First, she had to deal with what had happened.

At her front door, Sarah turned to Aaron. "Do you want to come in? The girls are at my mother's house, and we won't have to worry about disturbing them."

"Sure," said Aaron. "We didn't get much of a chance to talk at Jake's. Tell me about the new guy, Blake. He and Poppy seemed to have hit it off. I heard him say he might be looking for work. We always need people."

Sarah unlocked the door, and they went inside. Without the girls' presence, it seemed so quiet. So peaceful.

Aaron walked silently behind her as she went into the kitchen and snapped on the lights. Blinking at the brightness, she didn't notice that Aaron had come closer, and she was startled when he wrapped his arms around her.

She leaned against his chest loving the feel of him close to her. When she realized he was aroused, she stepped away.

He shot her a sad look. "Someday ..."

Feeling bad about her inability to simply let go of the past, she cupped his cheek in her hand. "It isn't fair of me to expect you not to date or see other women. I'm working on myself and my situation, but I don't know how long it will take for me to come to terms with what happened to Jesse."

"Just promise me you'll keep trying," said Aaron. He rubbed his hand through his long hair. "I think I should go."

Sarah swallowed hard. "I'll walk you to the door."

They kissed without lingering, then she stood aside while he left.

After she closed and locked the door, Sarah burst into tears. Looking around, she noticed the photograph of Jesse with the girls when they were infants. It was sitting on a table in the living room. That was before he began to spiral.

She marched over to it, and in a fit of anger, she threw it on the floor, shattering the glass.

Furious at him for what he'd done to them, she kicked at the frame.

When Sarah caught her breath, she stared at the mess on the floor. It was time to clean out her house and get rid of her past. She'd already removed photographs of Jesse's parents from the grouping she'd created right after she and Jesse were married. After his parents had accused her of being at fault for how she'd handled Jesse's depression, she couldn't bear to look at their faces.

She stood staring at nothing, her fists clenched. All of a sudden, she screamed into the empty space, "Okay! I get it! Time to forgive myself!"

She put on some rock music and danced until she could hardly move, anything to get rid of her pent-up feelings. When she couldn't get her breath, she clenched her sides, then collapsed on the couch laughing until she burst into loud, heartfelt sobs. Her body began to shake, almost as if she was in shock, and she wrapped herself in the soft throw she'd hung on the back of the couch.

When her sobbing finally stopped, she lay back on the cushions and stared at the ceiling, feeling too weak to move. But her thoughts kept circling in her head. She'd tried to get help for Jesse, but after a few sessions with a doctor he didn't like, he refused to find another. And the medicine he was supposed to take was sometimes, but not always, taken. And other forbidden ones were taken in its place. All this while she was coping with two babies alone when Jesse disappeared for long periods of time or sat refusing to move from his favorite chair to help her.

Even the morning of the day he died, he'd lied to her and said he was feeling better. It wasn't until late afternoon that she realized something was terribly wrong. She had her neighbor watch the babies, and following her instincts, got in her car. She found his truck at the wooded park at the edge of the town. Their special place.

Unaware she was crying, she'd run into the woods and followed their favorite path until she found him. He'd used a gun to the head to end his life. Even now, thinking of it, her stomach turned. She drew deep breaths to steady herself.

Sarah finally forced herself to her feet, intent on following her new plan. She went to her bedroom and packed away the jewelry Jesse had given her. The girls might enjoy having those pieces when they were older. She faced her closet and her bureau. If she was ever going to free herself from the guilt and pain, it was time to clear them of certain items that reminded her of Jesse. She looked at the things she'd brought to Lilac Lake with her. The first to go was a blue dress that he'd loved seeing her wear.

By the time she was through cleaning out both the closet and her bureau, she had a large collection to give to charity. She'd changed her bedding when she moved back home, but looking at it now, she realized she'd picked out something Jesse would have liked. Tomorrow, she'd drive to a Target and get something different, something that reminded her of happier days in Lilac Lake, something feminine.

Exhausted, she looked at the clock, surprised to see it was after two a.m.

She peeled off her clothes and climbed into bed, still wearing her underwear, too tired to do more.

CHAPTER NINE

As soon as Sarah woke up in the morning, feeling groggy from a restless sleep, she lay in bed, planning her day. From this moment on, she was going to make her life her own. First, she needed to call her mother.

Sarah got out of bed, made herself a cup of coffee, and then picked up her phone. She was tired of listening to other people tell her what she should and should not do.

“Hi, Mom. I was wondering if you could keep the girls with you all day for me. I have a number of projects to take care of, and I can’t do them if they’re with me.”

“Of course, dear,” said her mother. “The girls have had a delightful time playing ‘dress-up.’ And I can take them to the movies this afternoon. Even if they can’t sit still for most of the show, it will be something different for them, and it will get me out of the house.”

“Thanks. You don’t know how much I appreciate it,” gushed Sarah. “You’re the best Mimi ever.”

Her mother laughed. “It’s exhausting work, but I love them so much. What are you going to be doing?"

"We’ll talk later. I’m about to leave the house now,” she fibbed. She didn’t want anyone to interfere with her day.

Sarah fixed herself a slice of wheat toast and another cup of coffee and sat down to write a list of things to get done. Just before she left the kitchen to take a shower, she made a phone call to Gage Martens, a local veterinarian.

Satisfied that she was ready to begin her day, Sarah showered and dressed, then headed out.

Her first stop was to visit Gage. He lived on a small farm outside of town and was in charge of the animal rescue center. She'd always wanted a dog. The girls had been asking for one, and now was the time to make her move. Jesse had refused to let her have a dog in the house. But with her new attitude toward her life, nobody could stop her.

Gage was fairly new to town, and with his hot body, brown hair, and butterscotch eyes, he had most eligible females suddenly thinking of owning a pet.

Sarah drove into the parking lot of the animal rescue center feeling optimistic. Gage had encouraged her to think of an older dog, not a puppy, and had told her he had one in mind.

She got out of the car and headed inside. The noise of barking dogs hit her ears, and she wondered if she should've asked about a cat instead.

But when Gage walked into the waiting area with a golden retriever on a leash, she knew she'd been right.

"Hello," said Gage. "Meet Luke. He's five years old and is as easygoing as a dog can be. His owner, a single woman, was heartbroken to have to leave him behind looking for a new home, but she's unexpectedly moving to New York City and couldn't take the dog with her. I assured her I'd find a good home for him."

Sarah knelt on the floor and called softly to Luke to come. He, not she, would decide if he was right for them.

Gage let go of the leash and Luke ambled over to her, sniffed her hand, and then moved closer. Tearing up, Sarah said softly, "I have two little girls just waiting for someone like you. Me, too."

He seemed to know what she was saying, swiped her cheek with his tongue, and then lay down in front of her, staring up at her with warm brown eyes.

Sarah threw her arms around his neck, and he inched closer, wagging his tail.

"He's beautiful," said Sarah, smiling up at Gage before rising.

Luke sat at her feet, looking up at her with a hopeful expression as he wagged his tail.

"Do you want to come home with me?" Sarah said.

Luke barked.

"Well, that's settled then," said Gage, pleased. "He's chipped, neutered, housebroken, and had all his shots. I've checked him over carefully, and he is in perfect health and ready to go."

"I'll go ahead and sign papers and pay. But I need you to keep him here until later today. Is that possible? I want to get everything ready at home for him. Did his owner leave any of his favorite things here?"

Gage chuckled. "Oh, yes. He has a special blanket he sleeps on and a few favorite toys. But it wouldn't hurt to get some things of your own to help make the transition. You told me you have a fenced yard and will make sure he gets proper exercise."

"Oh, yes," she said.

"One more thing, which is why I think he's perfect for you. He was used to going to the owner's office with her. He might want to go to work with you. Is that something you'd consider doing with him?"

"Yes," Sarah exclaimed. "That would be fun. He'd have plenty of space there, and I'm sure the customers would like him."

"That's what I figured," said Gage, giving her a satisfied grin. "He's a beautifully trained dog, and with his personality, he should make the transition easily."

After signing papers and paying the fee, Sarah patted Luke on the head. "Don't worry, boy, I'll be back to take you home. I know two little girls who are going to be thrilled."

Luke whined and wagged his tail, and though Sarah wished she could take him with her, she had to make sure she and the girls were ready for him.

Her second stop was the charity store, where she dropped off the bags of items that she'd decided to get rid of. She reminded herself that it was another way to start fresh.

Then Sarah headed out to do some shopping. She had some money saved up for a weekend escape she'd promised herself, but decided this was a better way to spend it.

Later, she put the last of her shopping bags into the back of the car and headed home to put it all in place. When she'd made the move to town, she'd sentimentally clung to furnishings and decorative items from her marriage. Now, they, too, would be given to charity. It was, as she repeated to herself, time for something new.

Smiling at the idea, Sarah stopped at the animal shelter and picked up Luke who happily jumped into her car. She wanted him to have time to get used to the house before the girls came home.

As she drove, she couldn't help laughing. Luke sat up in

the seat looking ahead as if he was her backseat driver.

"Ah, Luke. You're going to be exactly what our little family needs," she said, pulling into her driveway.

Sarah opened the back door of the car and let him out, giving him a few moments on the leash to sniff around the small front yard before leading him inside the house and then outside to the back yard.

She left the sliding glass door in the kitchen open so Luke could come and go as he wished. Then she went to the car to get her purchases.

After several trips, she was ready to begin work inside.

The first thing she did was to wash the quilt covering her bed so it could be given away, along with the two decorative matching pillows. She put the bedside lamp into a box, to be replaced with the new contemporary lamp that better matched the pale-rose linen duvet and flowery shams.

She'd splurged and bought new bath towels to match the color-scheme of the bedding, The old towels were in excellent shape and could be used in the girls' bathroom.

In the living room, she changed a few things around, replaced other pieces like bowls that had no meaning, added baskets to hold books and other items the girls used, and put a new silk plant in a corner to dress up the room.

While she was working, Luke came inside. Sarah pulled a new dog bed out of a bag and looking at him, she said, "Shall we put this in the kitchen where you can see everything?"

He followed her as she placed it by the stationary end of the sliding-glass door. "There. You have some sunshine. What do you think?"

Luke wagged his tail and sniffed it carefully before turning around and around and lying down in it.

She got out dog dishes for him and filled one with water, putting it in an open space at the end of the counter. She watched him lick some water and then he looked up at her, wagging his tail.

"Oh, Luke. You're going to have so much love here in your new home." She rubbed his ears, and chuckled when he gave her a doggy smile.

She went outside with him and watched as he sniffed every corner of the yard. He went over to the swing set near the house and sniffed it too.

"The girls are going to love you," said Sarah. "I'm going to get them now. Come. You need to wait inside until I bring them to you."

Sarah cleaned up the mess in the living room, closed the doors to her bedroom, told Luke she'd be right back, and went to the car to pick up the girls.

On the way home, both girls were talking at once. "What's the surprise? Is it big? No, it's small, isn't it?

"I want to see it first," said Mia, uncharacteristically selfish.

"The surprise is for all of us to share. His name is Luke, and he's a big dog you'll love. He's very friendly and very loving. You must be kind to him."

"A dog! Really?" said Emily, bursting into tears. "We've always wanted a dog."

"He's ours?" asked Mia.

"Yes, his name is Luke. I'm telling you now so when you come into the house, you'll allow him time to meet you. He's lived with someone else. We're giving him a new home. We need to be very gentle, very kind to him. Understand?"

She pulled into the driveway and looked in the rearview mirror for their agreement.

Both girls were nodding their heads, looking serious.

"Okay," said Sarah. "Please follow me to the front door. We'll greet him there."

"Hurry," said Emily tugging Sarah's hand.

The girls stood quietly behind her as she unlocked the door. When she opened it, Luke was at the door growling softly.

When he saw her, he wiggled his tail, licked her hand, and then, eying the girls carefully, he went over to them and sniffed them.

"He's yellow," said Mia.

"And big," Emily said, holding out her hand to him.

Mia patted him on the head. Then Emily.

Luke wagged his tail and pranced around them in excitement as they walked into the living room. But there was nothing threatening about him.

"Why don't you girls sit on the floor and let him come to you?" said Sarah, content with how things were going.

She stood by, watching carefully to see that the girls were careful with him, and he remained content to see them.

"I love him already," said Mia, patting Luke's head. He was lying between the girls, allowing them to pet him.

"I love him more," Emily said, and Sarah realized she'd been smart to go with an older dog rather than having two kittens, as she'd first thought.

"Okay, why don't you take Luke out to the backyard so he can play," said Sarah, making sure all three were happily active before starting to fix dinner.

Looking around, seeing that some of her wedding gifts were relegated to giveaways, Sarah let out a sigh of satisfaction. She felt freer to have them gone. She and Jesse had had some good times in the beginning. She understood that. But it was time to set even those memories aside if she was going to move forward.

After the excitement of playing outside with the dog fizzled, the girls came inside.

"Okay, you girls can help me feed the dog," said Sarah, "and then it will be time for dinner."

From the refrigerator, Sarah pulled out the dog food Gage had told her to buy and sprinkled the proper amount of food into a bowl. "Dr. Martens told me Luke might be too excited about being here to eat much. Let's see."

Sarah put the dish of food down next to the water dish, and the girls huddled close by.

"Give him some space. Dogs don't like to be crowded when they're eating."

Left alone, Luke dug into his food.

"Good job," said Emily when the dog had finished.

"All gone," Mia said, patting him on the head.

"Okay, now it's time for us to eat. Wash your hands and climb up in your seats," said Sarah. "We're having your favorite—spaghetti."

"Luke, lie down in your bed," said Sarah, hoping it was a command he understood.

He looked at her and then did as she said.

"Good dog," cooed Sarah. She served their meal and then sat at the table, unusually hungry after her busy day. Gage had said he was an excellent dog, but having him with them was much easier than she'd thought.

"Can Luke sleep with me?" asked Mia.

"No, he's going to sleep with me," Emily said.

"I think he should sleep on the floor between your beds. That's fair," said Sarah. "But if he wants to choose somewhere else, we'll let him. We want him to be comfortable, right? It's bath time. You have school tomorrow, and we want to be ready."

"Can Luke come with us?" asked Emily.

"Let's let him decide what he wants to do and where he wants to be," said Sarah. The dog hadn't had much rest since the girls came home.

To the girls' delight, Luke was curious enough to walk into the bathroom and sit nearby to watch them as they played in the tub.

And later, when Sarah led the girls into their bedroom, he followed them. And after each girl had climbed into her bed, Luke lay down on the rug between their beds and stayed there as Sarah read to the girls and even after Sarah kissed the girls and headed for the door.

She left the door open a crack as usual. If Luke wanted to leave, he could.

As she was cleaning the kitchen and preparing snacks for the girls for the next day, she was surprised by a phone call from Gage.

"Hi, Sarah. I'm just calling to see how my latest placement is going. Is Luke happy there? Getting along with the children?"

"He's a dream dog," said Sarah. "Thank you so much. He's fitting in fine with the family. He ate all his dinner and is now sleeping on the rug between the girls' beds. We're thrilled to have him."

"I'm glad to hear it. As you can imagine, his previous owner was very sad to have to let him go. But I promised her I'd see that he went to a good home. I almost took him myself, but I already have two dogs of my own."

"I appreciate your letting us have him," said Sarah. "Are you going to be at Jake's this week?"

"I'm going to try," said Gage. "Glad things are working out for you and the dog. See you later. If you have any questions for me, please feel free to call."

"Thanks," said Sarah, just as the doorbell rang. She clicked off the call and hurried to the door, hoping not to disturb the girls.

Before she could get there, a streak of yellow raced by her and stood guard at the door.

She patted Luke's head. "It's okay. It's just my friends."

She opened the door and greeted Misty and Hazel. "Come on in and meet Luke, our new dog."

Luke stood at Sarah's side and allowed the other women to pat him, but he didn't seem to relax until Sarah had hugged each of her friends.

She led them into the kitchen. "How about a cup of hot tea?"

"Sounds delicious," said Hazel. "Wait a minute. You've been redecorating your living room. It looks nice."

"And I've worked on my bedroom. Come see what I've done." She led them away from the girls' room to the master bedroom.

"Wow!" said Misty. "It looks like a photo for Pottery Barn."

"Gorgeous," said Hazel. "So feminine."

"That was the purpose," said Sarah. She turned to two of the people she trusted the most. "I've had a breakthrough of sorts. Come to the kitchen and I'll tell you all about it."

After fixing tea, the women helped themselves to it and then sat at the table.

"Okay, what's going on? Are you alright?" asked Misty, giving her a steady look.

"Yes, making physical changes is something. But how about you?" Hazel asked.

"You know all about Jesse's death and the scars it left on me," Sarah began. "Mostly because of guilt. Last night, after Aaron walked me home, I realized I had to make some changes. Do things my way and for myself and my girls." She patted Luke on the head.

"The dog?" said Misty.

"I've always wanted a dog, but Jesse wouldn't let me have one. He said it took too much work." She rubbed Luke's ears. "Gage helped choose this dog for me. The girls love him, and I feel safe having him around. His previous owner took him to work. I'm going to try that too."

"And the decorating?" asked Hazel.

"I'm giving away some of the wedding gifts we were given, gotten rid of things that remind me of Jesse. Cleaned house of him, so to speak. The pleasant memories will always be part of me, but the others were weighing me down."

"Does this have anything to do with Aaron?" Misty asked, giving her a searching look.

Sarah felt heat rise to her cheeks. "I'm working on making positive changes in my life. Healing wounds. We were together in high school. Things are a lot different now, but I'd like to start over with him. It'll take baby steps, but I'm willing to try. And he's being patient."

"He adores you," said Misty. "He always has."

"He's different from any man I've ever known, quite spiritual. There's something that binds us together. I want to try to move forward."

Misty got out of her chair and hugged her. "I'm proud of you, Sarah. You've taken some major steps in that direction."

"Yes, girl, we're here for you," said Hazel. "It would be a shame not to see where this could take you."

Sarah remembered Aaron's sweet words about harvesting their love and agreed.

CHAPTER TEN

The next morning, Sarah felt something cold touch her hand. She jerked her hand away and sat up in bed holding back a scream. It took her a moment to realize Luke was standing by her bed looking at her curiously.

"Oh, Luke," she said. "Do you need to go outside?"

His ears perked up at the word "outside", and he darted towards the door.

Sarah quickly got up, threw her robe on, and hurried to the sliding door in the kitchen, thankful she could let him out this way.

She stood at the door and gazed at the fenced backyard. Beyond it, through the trees, she could see the sparkle of sunlight on the river. The leaves on the trees were changing into a bright red color that seemed magical. No wonder "leaf peepers" flocked to New Hampshire to see colors like this.

Luke returned to her wagging his tail. She gazed at his face seeing how relieved he seemed to be out of the shelter and at her home. Sarah was rubbing his ears and talking softly to him, when the girls raced into the kitchen.

"There you are, Luke!" Mia cried.

Emily hugged him. "We thought you went away."

"He slept with you girls through the night but had to go outside this morning. Don't worry. He's not going away. He's living with us for real." She hugged each girl. "Who wants waffles for breakfast?"

Laughing at the chorus of "me!" Sarah left the girls petting Luke and went to get breakfast ready. She was anxious to see how well Luke would do at work. If he behaved properly, it would be nice to have him around the store. Thinking of him as part of the family, she was very happy she'd chosen to adopt him. He was already a bright light in their lives.

Later, the girls, Luke, and Sarah left the house. Both girls held onto Luke's leash as they walked to preschool. Luke was as well trained as Gage had told her. He paced his steps to match those of the girls, and though he stopped a few times to sniff at the grass or trees, he was careful about staying with them.

"Can we bring him inside preschool? Emily asked.

"We'll let him see where you go to school, and then he's coming to work with me," said Sarah. It did her heart good to see how loving the girls were with the dog.

The teachers at the preschool greeted them warmly and spent some time allowing the other children to pet Luke, one by one. Luke took it all in stride, and Sarah wondered if he'd been trained to be a therapy dog. It seemed like it.

When it was time for them to leave, Sarah kissed the girls and led Luke away.

On a whim, she decided to walk over to the park that David Graham had installed in memory of his sister. It was a couple of blocks over from Main Street but not so far out of the way to delay her arrival at the store for too long.

When they got to the small park, Sarah walked over to a bench and sat down. The garden was well maintained by

David and the landscaping company he owned with his father. Flower beds were beautifully planted and cared for, making it the perfect spot for her to sit and contemplate her latest attempts to heal from Jesse's suicide.

Luke sniffed around, going only as far as his leash allowed, before sitting beside the bench.

Sarah gazed at the flower beds lining the lot. The different colored mums and other flowers made a nice pattern. She thought of the memorial service Jesse's parents had insisted on holding at their local Baptist church. She'd been too hurt, confused, and angry to do more than go through the motions. Here, sitting in this simple garden, she felt closer to Jesse than she had since then. It was important to think of the happy times with him and leave the rest behind. If she wanted to have a new life. it wouldn't do to her good to hang onto the horrible past.

Feeling better, she left the garden and walked over to Main Street toward the café for coffee to take with her to work.

She was standing across the street from the café when Aaron emerged from it. Seeing her, he waved and went to his truck.

Sarah hurried over to him, hoping to catch him before he pulled away.

When he saw her approach, he stepped on the brakes. "Hey, there."

"Hi, Aaron, I want to apologize for the other night. I want you to know I've done a lot of thinking and have made some changes."

He looked down at Luke. "Did you get a dog?"

Sarah grinned. "Jesse would never let the girls and me have one. Meet Luke, one of the sweetest Golden Retrievers

I've ever met."

Luke lifted his head to smell Aaron's hands and turned to the two black Labs in the back of his truck.

"I bet the girls are thrilled to have him. Is he going to work with you?" Aaron asked.

"Yes. His previous owner used to take him to her job, and I think he'll do fine in the store. He's as calm and collected as any dog I've seen."

"Great," said Aaron.

Sarah paused and then blurted, "That's not the only change I've made. I've cleared a lot of things from the house, so I can make a new start." She looked at him for approval.

Aaron studied her, his dark eyes searching hers. "That's nice, but the real changes need to come from the inside. They need to bring you peace. I can't be the thing that makes you want to change things. That has to come from you."

Sarah stood back so he could pull the truck away from the curb. Her heart thumped with disappointment. She'd thought Aaron would be excited for her.

She went inside the café and ordered a cup of coffee to go and showed off Luke to her friends. Then she crossed the street to the store.

Inside, her father walked over to her. "This dog yours?" He petted Luke.

"This is Luke, the newest member of the family. He's around five years old and is well-trained. The girls and I have fallen in love with him. He's doing great with them and our house."

"Are you going to have him stay here while you work?" her father asked.

"Yes, whenever it's convenient. His former owner used to

take him to her job all the time. I thought he'd do well here at the store. I'll keep him in my office to start."

"It's fine by me. It'll give a friendly touch to the store. But if he becomes a nuisance of any kind, he goes."

"Fair enough. Thanks, Dad," said Sarah.

Sarah led Luke up the stairs to her office. They stopped outside her mother's door, and seeing that she was free, Sarah took Luke inside.

Her mother gazed at the dog with curiosity. "Who is this?"

"The newest member of the family. Meet Luke. The girls and I are in love with him."

"That's why I needed to watch Mia and Emily all day?" asked her mother with a bit of a frown on her face.

Sarah sat down and faced her mother. "I've been clearing out items that remind me too much of Jesse. I've put away jewelry for the girls to have later in their lives and made a big effort to move forward with my life by not being weighed down by grief and guilt. Jesse never allowed the girls and me to have a dog. And, Mom, it feels such a relief to be able to do things my way."

"You met up with Aaron on Thursday, right?" Her mother asked, giving her a penetrating stare. "Does this have anything to do with him?"

Sarah let out a long sigh. "I thought it did, but he told me that though the changes might be nice, the real changes have to come from within. I think I'll go back to the grief support group. I don't want to miss the chance to really heal."

"Oh, darling, that makes me so relieved. You deserve to be able to move ahead with your life. It's important to do it the right way." Her mother stood and gave her a hug.

###

When April arrived for work that afternoon, Sarah did a double take. Gone was the rather frumpy young girl of last week. Over the weekend, April had had her hair cut and colored and wore a cute turquoise turtleneck top over a pair of black leggings, and black ankle boots.

"April, you look fabulous! I love your hair and your new outfit. I almost wish you didn't need to change into your 'uniform'."

"Thanks. That means a lot. Lindsay Legget, the mean girl I told you about earlier, said I looked terrible, more like her mother than the other kids."

"Wow! That's an awful thing to say. She must be jealous," said Sarah, wondering why girls could be so mean to one another.

April shrugged. "I think she said that because Wyatt came over to me at school to tell me he liked the new look. Lindsay thinks she's the only one who should talk to him, that he's her property. Just because they're dating."

"Ah, so she's jealous. It's nice that Wyatt noticed you, but beware a girl like Lindsay."

"Yeah, she and her small group of girlfriends can be cruel. I usually stay away from them." Luke sat beside her wagging his tail and whining for attention. April turned to him. "Who's this?"

"Meet Luke, my new dog. He's friendly and very well behaved."

Luke stood and quieted with contentment as April rubbed his ears. "He's very nice."

Luke licked her hand, and April laughed. "Guess he likes me."

Sarah was gratified to see such a nice boost in April's confidence. "Time to change your clothes. We've got boxes to unload, and there's no way I want you to ruin your new clothes."

April laughed. "Okay, I'll be right back."

Later, Sarah and April were in the middle of unpacking boxes when Sarah asked her if she was willing to help out at the Halloween Walk.

"It would be a help to have you here. You could have fun dressing up and handing out candy to the kids who come through the store," said Sarah.

"Now that my dad is home, I'll do it," said April. "He and I have had a long talk, and we agreed to make our own decisions, not rely on my grandmother to tell us what to do. He's only been home a few days, but he's changed. I like it."

"That's wonderful," said Sarah. "Thanks for agreeing to help for Halloween. It's a big deal in town and thrilling for the younger kids."

"I didn't get to do much last year. I had to stay home to hand out candy to the kids in the neighborhood. So, this year will be fun. What should I dress up as?"

"Anything you want as long as it isn't too scary," said Sarah.

"Okay. I'll think of something," said April smiling.

Wyatt appeared. "Do you have anything heavy that I need to move for you? My work downstairs is done for the day."

Sarah noticed the way Wyatt was trying not to look at April and how he couldn't stop himself from doing so. Playing along with his request, she said, "Nothing heavy to move, but you can restock some of the shelves up here with items we just checked in."

"Okay, no problem. Glad to do it," said Wyatt.

April smiled at him, and his ears turned red. With his blond hair, blue eyes, and muscular body he was awfully cute.

Sarah showed Wyatt where to place things and then she went to her office so the two young people could be alone. April was fully capable of doing the work without Sarah's supervision. This would be a test for her.

Luke followed her into the office and lay down on the rug. But his ears continued to twitch as conversation between April and Wyatt took place.

Watching him, Sarah's lips curved. "Luke, you're the best dog ever."

He gazed up at her and thumped his tail against the rug.

She thought of all the changes in the last couple of days and was amazed at how normal her "new" life seemed.

Sarah got ready to attend the grief support group she'd signed up for. She was lucky she had parents who could watch the girls for a couple of hours while she went to it. They'd used babysitting as a lure to bring her back to town but were faithful about following through. The girls adored them and rightly so. They were wonderful grandparents.

It was a cool and rainy fall night. Sarah wished the girls and her babysitting father goodnight and then walked to her car parked in her driveway. She had a one-car garage that had some old furniture stored there. Unloading it was another project for her to do now that she could face making those changes.

She drove to the Unitarian Church sitting in the middle of town and parked. Sitting inside her car, she drew deep breaths. She was someone who held her feelings close to her. She'd tried the group right after she moved back to town but wasn't settled enough in her mind to want to confess a true part of her feelings. Now, she hoped she was ready.

Inside the church, in one of the social rooms, she found a small group of people and was surprised to see April's father there. The others appeared to be older. She unclasped her hands and realized this might be easier than she'd thought.

Blake gave her a nod in greeting, and she went and sat down in the empty chair beside him so she wouldn't have to stare at him from across the circle of chairs.

"I'm surprised to see you here," he said to her.

"It's been a while in coming, but I realize I need to do this. I like the idea that anything spoken here will be honored as confidential," said Sarah.

"Me, too," said Blake. "I've kept a lot of feelings stuffed inside, tried to escape it. But April needs her father, and I intend to stay."

"What will you do here?" asked Sarah. "Aaron and Brad Collister own the Meadows and are always in need of help if you have any skills they can use."

"I'm renting a house, but I intend to buy one in town. I could use their ideas for renovation," he said.

"Oh, in that case, you'll want to talk to Dani, Brad's wife. She's an architect and is fantastic at designing additions and upgrading homes. Have you found a house you like?"

"I have an idea I'm developing for housing," he said. "As far as a job is concerned, I have a degree in financial management and was doing that kind of work for a company outside Boston before my wife died, and then I sort of crashed and burned."

"Do you want to continue in that line of business?" asked Sarah.

"No," said Blake firmly. "I purposely chose to hit the road and get as far away from a corporate lifestyle as possible. Now, because of April, I want to be home with her every night. These are difficult years for any child, and she's had way too much to deal with. I thought it would be helpful for her to be with another woman, my mother. But as close as they sometimes are, April needs a different homelife." He shook his head. "I uprooted April from her school and handed her off to my mom and ran. I've been pretty screwed up."

An older woman entered the room and said, "Hello, everyone. I'm Dr. Ellen Fitzpatrick, your grief counselor. But please simply call me Ellen. I'm delighted to see so many of you here ready to navigate your losses."

She moved to one of the chairs in the circle. "This is a safe place for all of you. Like AA, we won't be sharing names with anyone outside the circle, and all information told here will be considered confidential. You wouldn't be here if you didn't want help coping with a loss of some kind. Feel free to share your thoughts, but kindness and respect are essential from all of us."

Sarah moved uncomfortably in her chair when Ellen continued. "Please, everyone, share your name and why you're here."

The person next to her began.

When it was Sarah's turn, she gripped her hands. "My name is Sarah. I'm here because my husband committed suicide almost two years ago and I'm still trying to cope with what happened."

Blake's turn was next. "Hi, everyone. I'm Blake. My wife was killed in a car accident with another man. They were running away together." He hesitated. "She was an addict, and he was her supplier."

Hearing the pain in his voice, Sarah's stomach clenched. No wonder the man had wanted to escape and hit the road himself. No other announcements were as surprising. Most of the other eight people were here for deaths of loved ones due to cancer and heart conditions. One woman announced her spouse had died from what she'd called simply old age.

Ellen guided them into discussions of survivor's guilt, typical angry reactions, and other responses. "All responses are acceptable. There's no judgement here."

When Ellen spoke to Sarah about the anger Sarah had worked on over the weekend, Ellen gave her a nod of approval. "It's okay to be angry. Especially when suicide has been committed. It leaves those left behind with penetrating questions about whether any of it was their fault."

"Can we ever know what truly goes on in another's mind?" asked Blake. "My wife left not only me but my daughter when she took off that day. I know she loved my daughter, but I guess she loved drugs more."

"Addiction is a topic unto itself," said Ellen. "I'm very sorry about your situation. Tell me how you're handling it."

"That's just it. I'm not handling it very well. I took off, too, leaving my daughter with my mother, coming back often to visit as often as I could while driving trucks for a living. I felt someone else would do a better job of parenting than I could because I couldn't even keep a wife. Guess that makes me an asshole."

"It makes you a hurting, confused person. I'm glad you're here. Have you talked to others about your feelings?" Ellen asked Blake.

"A counselor in Boston who I couldn't relate to. An older man who doesn't really understand the drug culture," Blake replied.

"We'll have plenty of time to delve into situations like this in the coming weeks. I've arranged to have a special speaker join us."

After a little more time, the meeting ended, and people stood around chatting and sipping punch and cookies.

Blake approached Sarah. "I'm sorry about your husband."

"And I'm sorry about your wife," Sarah said. She put a hand on his arm. "You're no asshole. Your daughter adores and respects you."

"She's something all right. With your help and Poppy's, April's coming out of her shell and beginning to find her place in school. Who's Wyatt?"

"A popular boy in high school who may have a crush on April. I must warn you, though, that his girlfriend, a student named Lindsay Legget, is very mean and won't like that idea at all."

"Am I making it up or was high school a lot easier back when I went to school than it is now?"

"It's always been a struggle, but with social media, it's much harder. I'm glad I don't have to be a high school student today," said Sarah.

"I'll protect my girl any way I can," said Blake with a look of resolution.

"That's sweet to hear," Sarah said. "Are you coming to Jake's on Thursday?"

Blake nodded. "Like you said, it's a great group of people. I'm meeting Poppy there."

"Poppy is one of the best. She's a wonderful addition to town. She came here to take care of a dying family member and has chosen to stay."

"Yes, I know. She's living in the family house that needs quite a bit of renovation. I'm thinking I may be able to help her. But please don't say a word to anyone about it," said Blake.

"I won't," Sarah answered, but her mind was spinning.

CHAPTER ELEVEN

THURSDAY EVENING, SARAH RODE TO JAKE'S WITH HAZEL.

"These events are lifesavers for me," Hazel said. "I'm hoping Gage will be there. He's someone I'm interested to get to know better."

"I like him. He was very helpful in my adopting Luke," said Sarah. She, herself, hoped to see Aaron. Surprisingly, she hadn't heard anything from him since they'd talked outside the café. This would be the last gathering before the town would be swept up with Halloween parties or, like her, ensuring the younger children had a wonderful time.

When Sarah and Hazel arrived at Jake's, their regular tables were pretty crowded. Sarah realized Aaron wasn't among them, and her heart fell.

Hazel went to sit by Gage, and Sarah found an empty chair by Blake, who was talking quietly to Poppy. She continued to look around the table.

Tessa gave her a little wave. "I had a great time with your friend, Aaron. He took me for a canoe ride on the lake like I asked him, and he saved my life. I'm not kidding. I'll never be able to thank him enough."

"What happened?" Sarah asked, forcing herself to speak calmly. *Aaron with Tessa?*

Tessa told the whole group how, after arranging for Aaron to spend the afternoon with her on the lake, she'd tried to switch places with him in the canoe and they'd tipped over. "Aaron jumped in and saved me because I wasn't wearing a life jacket. He was my hero, truly wonderful. I'd wanted a real experience with a real native and got it."

Sarah stared in disbelief hearing Tessa's words. *What had Aaron been thinking when he'd agreed to go out with her? Of all the people in the group, Tessa was the one person she didn't trust. There was something about her that didn't ring true. And that talk of a native? What was that all about?*

Now, Tessa was announcing that she was considering buying a house in The Meadows. *Did social directors make that much money?*

Sarah glanced at Melissa who was subtly shaking her head.

Frowning, Sarah looked up as Aaron walked over to the group and took the only empty seat left, the one next to Tessa.

He smiled at her and then look confused when Tessa beamed at him and said, "I told everyone how you saved me."

"What are you talking about?" asked Aaron.

"You know, after I tipped the canoe, you carried me to shore," said Tessa.

"You could have walked to shore yourself in the shallow water, but you flailed around so much it was quicker to just carry you. The water is cold this time of year." Though he spoke calmly, I could tell from the twitching of his left eye that he was very annoyed. Telling the truth was a basic moral code for him.

A little flustered, Tessa said, "Well, I was awfully glad you were there."

Gage took the following moment of quiet to ask, "How's Luke doing with you and the girls, Sarah."

"He's wonderful, the best dog ever," said Sarah.

"My Dachshund, Mindy, would tell you she was the best," said Whitney giving her a challenging look.

"How about my dog, Pirate?" teased Dani. "Aaron gave him to me from the pups he'd raised."

The earlier tension was broken by bouts of laughter as owners shared stories of their dogs.

"Gage, the competition is fierce. You might have more adoptions to make," said Hazel, grinning at him.

He returned her smile. "It's always a rewarding feeling to see an animal find a forever home."

"How about cats?" said Poppy. "My tiger is the sweetest."

Gage looked at Sarah. "The girls might like to have some kittens. I don't think Luke would be a problem with them."

Sarah laughed. "One change at a time." She couldn't help glancing at Aaron, but he was saying something to Tessa.

Seeing them together, Sarah stood. "I've got to be going. I'm glad we all had a chance to get together, so I can invite you to stop by the store for the Halloween celebrations we'll have going on. During and after the walk for the kids, we'll be offering drinks and hors d'oeuvres for the grown-ups."

"That sounds like fun," said Beth Beckman. Her husband, Garth, and his family owned Beckman Lumber. They had two children who would be old enough to love seeing all the sights.

Sarah and Hazel exchanged looks and she realized Hazel was glad to have some time with Gage without having to take Sarah home.

Just as she reached the front door to Jake's, Aaron came up behind her. "Wait. I didn't get a chance to talk to you. May I walk you home?"

"Okay, sure. The girls have a Halloween party at school

tomorrow, and I know we'll be up early. That's why I had to leave."

Aaron's dark gaze met her. "You don't have to explain to me. C'mon. Let's go."

Outside, the air smelled of leaves and smoke from fireplaces and something that was uniquely the lake.

They walked down the sidewalk keeping pace with one another. As they strode together, Sarah let out a sigh. It felt right to be with him. She realized how jealous she'd felt when Tessa started talking about her date with Aaron, and turned to look at him.

He swept her hand up in his. "How are those changes going?"

"I've decided to go back to my grief group."

"Khalil Gibran is famous for this quote: '*Yesterday is but today's memory, and tomorrow is today's dream.*' I've always liked it. Everyone needs a dream to move towards." He stopped and lifted her chin. "I have my dreams too."

Sarah closed her eyes as his arms wrapped around her. She clung to him, feeling as if he was the one person who'd understood better than anyone how she'd struggled.

When they pulled apart, she reached up and tucked a strand of dark hair behind his ear. "Do you remember our times together in high school? How unique they were?

"We're meant to be together. I knew it when we met. Who else would've accepted me so quickly?"

"Or me?" Sarah said. "We were an odd couple back then, so different from some of our friends. We both loved poetry and reading together and sometimes lying on the rock by the lake just listening to the sounds around us."

"You made me realize it was okay to be different. I love

the Collister family and am grateful to them. But it was you who made me feel as if I belonged here."

Sarah studied him, her heart pounding with promise. "I heard what you were telling me the other day about changes coming from within. I want you to know I'm really trying to let the past be today's memory and move forward."

"That's what I want for you," said Aaron.

Taking hold of her hand again, they walked in silence. As usual, words weren't necessary between them. It had always been that way.

The next morning, as Sarah had predicted, the girls were up early, excited to get into their costumes for the school's Halloween celebration. Emily had chosen to be a fairy. Mia wanted to be a chef.

"Let's eat a healthy breakfast and then you can get dressed. It's going to be a lot of fun today, but we must get off to a good start," said Sarah fully aware of what a sugary day it was going to be.

"Is Luke going to wear his special hat today?" asked Mia.

"No, that's for tomorrow at the store," said Sarah, chuckling when she noticed a look of what she thought of as relief cross Luke's face. The dog continued to show extraordinary patience with the girls.

Finally, after getting everything in order, costumes on the girls, and packing favorite vegetable treats for school, Sarah, Luke, and the girls left the house for school in her SUV.

The drop-off spot for the girls was filled with parents and over-excited children. Teachers, dressed as assorted characters, tried to make order out of chaos.

Grinning at some of the costumes everyone wore, Sarah was delighted that her mother had made the girls their costumes. Halloween was not her favorite holiday, and the thought of creating costumes was nightmarish.

Luke waited in the car, his nose pressed to the car window, as Sarah carried her treats inside.

When she returned, he wiggled with happiness. Loving the feeling of being special, she got in the car and accepted the licks he gave her on the cheek.

At the store, Sarah showed photos she'd taken of Mia and Emily in costume to both her parents. "It's such an exciting time for them. Thank you, Mom, for making their costumes. They looked adorable."

Her mother placed an arm around Sarah. "I'm delighted that you're back in town with the girls. It's where you belong."

"Thanks. I think so, too. I've invited all my friends to stop by tomorrow for the Halloween Walk. I told them we'd have drinks and hors d'oeuvres for the adults."

"We're usually not that fancy, but I'll order some appetizers from the café. They've posted a sign about ordering treats. Hopefully, I'm not too late."

"It should be a fun event. April is going to be a big help."

"She's a lovely girl. I see such big changes in her already. And now that her father is staying in town, I think she'll find she'll fit in better knowing it's permanent."

"Yes, me, too," said Sarah, still intrigued about some of Blake's plans.

###

In preparation for the celebration, Sarah and her father moved things around in the store to make room for visitors by expanding the check-out area. They set up two cornhole games in the front display window of the store. That's where kids would play the game and win prizes. It would be fun for them, and entertaining for the people watching them from outside, where a refreshment stand was set up. Both the check-out area and the stand would have adult beverages as well as treats for any age.

Bullard's Hardware store wasn't the only store doing this. Main Street would be closed to traffic by late afternoon so all could participate. Even the tiniest of shops would have decorated windows and treats to give away. Whitney's husband, Nick, would be on patrol with his staff, to make sure the safety of the group was assured.

Later, Sarah went home to make sure her girls were taking a nap. Hazel had offered to watch them, but Sarah knew if they didn't rest before the event, they'd turn into cranky monsters.

At the front door, Hazel greeted her with a finger to her lips.

"They're sleeping?" whispered Sarah, hugging Hazel. "Thank you." She held up a brown bag. "I brought you a sandwich, your favorite chicken one, from the café. Want to sit and have lunch with me?"

"Thanks. I'd love to." Hazel beamed at her. "Gage asked me to join him tonight for the festivities. I'm so excited."

"Sweet," said Sarah. "What happened after I left the group at Jake's the other night?"

"Everyone is excited about the Halloween events. Tessa pouted because she had to work at the Inn. But she said she'd come to town as soon as she could. Most everyone else is planning on being there, including Aaron." Hazel gave her a penetrating look. "What's going on with him and Tessa? It all seemed weird to me."

"I don't think it's serious," said Sarah. "She really exaggerated the episode on the lake. It isn't the only time she's done that. Now, she's talking about buying a home at The Meadows?"

"I don't understand. Is she rich?" asked Hazel. "She's got to have a story behind her."

"I think so too, but I'm not going to worry about it. I have a feeling she's here to look for a man. You must admit, the group of single men here may be small, but they're all likeable. And successful, in their own way."

"True. Maybe that blurb on social media about great towns for singles has something to do with her wanting to be here."

"The one on Instagram?" Sarah asked. "I heard about it but never saw it."

"Whatever the reason, I'm going to keep an eye on Tessa," said Hazel. "Now, let me tell you about Gage." A huge smile spread across her face. "He walked me to my car, and he kissed me ."

"And?"

"And it was nice," said Hazel. "We agreed we'd meet up tonight for the festivities."

"He seems like a really sweet guy," said Sarah. "He was dating someone before he moved here. But I don't know anything about it."

"I intend to find out," said Hazel. "My mother would like the idea of me dating a doctor."

Her eyes twinkled with humor. "She doesn't have to know all his patients are animals."

They laughed together.

After Hazel left, Sarah went to lay down. She liked being by herself, thinking about her life, her plans, her determination to embrace thinking of herself in a completely different way.

CHAPTER TWELVE

SARAH STOOD OUTSIDE THE STORE GREETING THE CHILDREN and their parents. Wearing a black gown and a witch's hat with a sprig of flowers sewn onto it, she handed the children a candy bar and invited their parents to have refreshments while April and Wyatt, dressed alike, ushered the kids who were old enough inside for games.

April and Wyatt had decided to dress as construction workers, with aprons, tool belts, baseball caps, and their store T-shirts. It was the perfect way to appear as helpers. Sarah had a suspicion her mother had helped them make that decision.

Looking at the constant stream of families walking down Main Street, Sarah was touched. The Halloween Walk, unlike the Holiday Walk and Festival, was low key, more a small town affair just for locals. She liked it that way. Christmas was a time to draw people to town to celebrate. This quieter scene brought people in town together.

Her mother came out front to take Sarah's place so she could walk along Main Street with her girls.

Each storefront window was filled with decorations among their offerings. Halloween flags, fall flowers, orange and black ribbons wrapped around the streetlight poles, all lent a festive look to the street. For children like Mia and Emily, it was a fairyland. That, and receiving the treats from people at various locations was a child's dream come true.

At Poppy's store, Sarah accepted a cup of wine from Blake, who was helping Poppy out. Smiling, she thanked him and oversaw the treats handed to the girls. Poppy was adorably dressed like a kitty cat, complete with a whiskered half-mask. Blake wore a pumpkin hat.

"I hope you're enjoying your first Halloween Walk," Sarah said to Blake. "April is doing a fantastic job at my store."

He chuckled. "I've never seen anything quite like it, but it's nice."

"Have fun," she said, leading the girls next door to the flower shop.

There the girls were delighted to get a flower pinned onto their costumes.

When they returned to the hardware store, Sarah's mother took the girls inside so they could watch the other kids playing games in the window.

By about eight o'clock, the younger children were ready to go home. Sarah said goodbye to her parents, thanked the staff members who'd helped out at the store, and headed home with the girls.

"There you are!" came a familiar voice.

Sarah turned to find Aaron walking toward them.

The girls jumped up and down saying, "Look what I got!"

Aaron smiled at Sarah and spent some time with the girls while they showed him their treats and prizes.

Watching him, she was touched by how kind and gentle he was with them.

"Carry me," said Mia. "I'm too tired to walk."

Aaron glanced at Sarah and then said, "Okay. I can take one of you."

"I'll take the other," said Sarah.

With a child in his arms, Aaron walked steadily beside Sarah, keeping the conversation light.

Before they even reached Sarah's house, both children fell asleep.

"Guess the celebration was a success," said Aaron.

"It'll take more than one day for them to recover from the excitement and sugar, but it was worth it. Everyone pitched in to make it a nice, safe Halloween for the kids. Will you come inside? I'm ready for a glass of wine and some peaceful moments."

"Sure. I'm glad I ran into you. I was late getting to the Walk. I'd promised Whitney and Nick that I'd help them by passing out candy at their house while Nick worked and Whitney took Timothy out to see the sights."

"I love that everyone pitches in to make it a special event for the kids," said Sarah, patting Luke on the head after she unlocked the front door.

Inside she led Aaron to the girls' room to put them down for the night. This was one time they could skip brushing their teeth. She took off their shoes and got them out of their costumes and then covered them up.

Aaron stood by watching her. "You've got this down to a routine. Very impressive."

Chuckling, she said, "I had to learn how to handle two babies pretty quickly. C'mon. It's a nice night. We can sit on the deck."

In the kitchen, Aaron opened the bottle of wine she handed him. "I'll be right back. I have something to show you."

She returned to the kitchen to find him already outside on the deck. She turned the deck lights on low, then took her seat, and lifted her glass. "Here's to our friendship. It goes back quite a way." She handed him the photograph she'd found recently.

"What's this?"

"It's a picture of us lying on a towel on the grass at the Lilac Lake Cottage before the Gilford girls fixed it up. We're facing one another smiling and there's a poetry book open. I remember that day so well."

"Wasn't that the first time we kissed?" Aaron asked.

Sarah nodded. "We've always been such good friends, even when it became a little more than that."

"Yes, I know," Aaron said quietly.

"Saying goodbye to you on my way to college was one of the hardest times ever," said Sarah. "But when I came back home for Thanksgiving break, you'd already moved on."

"Not exactly. I was dating casually, but it was nothing serious. Just killing time until you came home again. And then you and Jesse became a couple."

"Jesse and I should've waited before we married," Sarah said, not for the first time. "But here you and I are now, still friends. You have no idea how much that means to me."

"You know how I feel."

"For the first time since Jesse killed himself, I'm optimistic about the future, excited to see how things unfold." Sarah gave Aaron a steady look, hoping he'd see how much she cared.

But he'd turned and was staring out at the woods and the river beyond them. When he faced her, he said, "I was lucky you understood me when we first met. It was weird for a big kid like me to play football and spend time reading poetry and enjoying other things guys my age weren't doing. You know, like taking long walks in nature."

"You told me you did some of those things to honor your mother and what she taught you," said Sarah. "That made you very special in my eyes."

"My mother would've liked you," said Aaron. "She would tell me you and I knew one another in a past lifetime."

"I sometimes think that too," said Sarah. "That's why I don't understand why we seemed to drift apart so quickly after high school."

"It wasn't our time," said Aaron, his dark eyes focused on her.

"And now?" she asked.

"We shall see," Aaron said. "We'll know when it is."

They sipped their wine in quiet and stared out at the woods, hearing the sounds of night creatures in the rustle of leaves, the cries of an owl.

Sarah took a deep breath and leaned against the back of her deck chair. Just spending time like this with Aaron was as pleasant as it had always been.

"Do you want children of your own someday?" Sarah asked.

He turned to her. "Yes, as many as we desire together."

"I'm glad," Sarah said and let that idea settle between them.

"I'll be going away for a few days," said Aaron. "At this time of year, I usually take time to go visit my grandfather who is living with the Abenaki tribe near the Canadian border. It's a promise I keep for my mother. It's where I grew up."

"It's important that you do that," said Sarah.

"Yes, though we're busy at work, I need to go before the winter weather arrives and hunting season starts for me."

"I'd forgotten you lead hunters into the mountains during that time," said Sarah.

"Hunting is a good sport but only if you're respectful to the animals you kill. I like to teach hunters how to take care of the bodies correctly, so it benefits other creatures."

Thinking of Tessa's remarks about wanting to be with a real native, Sarah's stomach twisted. There was so much more to Aaron than a large, fit, handsome man who wore his dark hair loose or tied back.

"I'm glad I found you for a friend," said Sarah. "It still means a lot to me."

"I know," Aaron said, tugging on her hand until she rose and climbed into his lap, like she'd done in the past.

She leaned her head against his broad chest and let out a long satisfied sigh. She'd made a lot of progress in the last couple of weeks. She'd work on herself until she was ready for much more with Aaron. He was her home.

CHAPTER THIRTEEN

The next morning, Sunday, Sarah took the girls to the store with her while she helped to clean and straighten from the Halloween festivities. As she swept and put items back in place, the girls played the toss game, which she'd taken out of the window.

April showed up as expected, and together they worked on putting a fall display in the front window. In a couple of weeks, they'd turn it into a Christmas window, but for now, she liked the transition to fall items.

During a break, Sarah said, "Did you have fun last night? You did a terrific job here at the store."

April made a face and shrugged. "Wyatt asked me to go with him to meet some friends who were having a party. Lindsay got really mad when she saw us, but Wyatt told her to stop making nasty comments about me. One of the other girls was nice to me, though, and I think I might've made a new friend."

"I'm glad to hear it," Sarah said. "It's tough when someone picks on you. The best advice I have is to ignore it. It becomes ineffective if there's no reaction."

April's eyes rounded. "Were you bullied in high school?"

"Not really," said Sarah, "because we grew up together and learned we all were different. Mrs. Genie Wittner, the former owner of the Lilac Lake Inn and a well-respected woman in town, made it a point to befriend us all, and it was she who made sure no one was mistreated."

"That's nice," said April.

"I wasn't the most popular girl in high school but I had friends even though I pretty much stayed to myself, and was busy working at the store but."

"My job here is very important to me," said April. "Wyatt would never have noticed me without my working here."

"That's a win-win, then," said Sarah, giving April an encouraging pat on the back.

While Sarah worked on tallying sales figures for Saturday, April played with the girls.

Mia and Emily loved having April help them.

Even though the store was closed, someone rang the bell to be let inside. Curious, Sarah went to the front of the store and saw Blake standing outside.

She opened the door. "April is still working here with me, but come inside."

"I just wanted to tell her that I was going to be late taking her out to lunch. Poppy and I are meeting with a realtor."

At my look of surprise, he continued. "You know that idea I had for a house? Poppy doesn't want to stay in her large Victorian house by herself and can't afford to pay for the upgrades it needs. So, we made a deal. I'll buy the house from her and fix it up, and she's going to move into Misty Gilford's cabin because Misty is moving in with David Graham." He chuckled. "How's that for a lot of cooperation?"

"It sounds perfect to me," said Sarah. "And that's why you

wanted to talk to Dani and Collister Construction?"

"Yes. I plan on doing a lot of work myself, but I need them to guide me. Once this deal goes through, I'll be in touch with Dani, as you suggested. I want to open up the interior and make some other changes without destroying the character of the house."

"Dani is an excellent architect, and the house is in a superb location," said Sarah. "I'm sure Poppy is thrilled with the arrangements."

"She is," said Blake. "She and I have hit it off, and it's been nice for both of us."

"Oh, yes," said Sarah, loving how this small-town living worked out so well for some people.

"Hi, Dad," said April walking toward them.

"I'll leave you two alone," Sarah said. "I'd better check on the girls."

Sarah found Mia and Emily in the nail aisle. They'd removed two boxes of box nails off the shelf and were sitting on the floor making designs with the nails they'd dumped on the floor. She whipped out her phone and took a picture of them to send to Dani, hoping she'd see how clever her girls were. Dani doted on them.

After they'd cleaned up, Sarah told the girls she'd take them to the café for lunch.

Excited, they headed for the door.

At the café, Sarah and the girls were shown to a booth, where she could look at the other people inside. She was glad to see how crowded it was. It was so much more than a place where one could get excellent food. It was where you could meet up with neighbors and friends.

Several people waved to her as she and the girls ate. A couple of people walked over to their table to talk to her.

Sarah left the store feeling as if she'd been hugged by the entire town. It prompted her to go home and start cleaning out the garage while the girls lay down for a post-holiday rest.

At home, after getting the girls settled on their beds reading, she went out to the garage. It was filled with several pieces of furniture she couldn't use in the rental cabin. As she hauled them out to the driveway, she realized she never wanted to use them again.

Sarah made another pile of things next to the furniture to be given to charity. The garage had come with built in shelves along the back wall, and she used this to place the things she wanted to keep. Tools sat in another section. Brooms, rakes, and other gardening items she'd kept were stored appropriately.

Sweating from the exercise, Sarah stood back filled with satisfaction. Now, in addition to getting rid of things she no longer needed or wanted, her car could sit inside the garage during the winter months.

She realized she'd wallowed in self-pity in the past but was now moving ahead in a positive way. The house truly was becoming hers without the items from her years with Jesse keeping her bound to them.

Mia came out of the house and trotted over to her. "Emily and I are done resting."

"Okay," said Sarah, checking her watch. "It's late. Let me make a phone call, and then I'll play a game of Candyland with you like I promised."

Inside, Sarah called Goodwill to arrange a pickup and

then resolutely sat on the living room floor with the girls to play one of their favorite games. Luke lay beside them content to watch.

That night, Sarah lay in bed thinking of everything that had happened over the past few days. As hectic as it was, she'd come a long way in becoming the person she wanted to be. Seeing Aaron, and spending time with him remembering their high school years together, had reminded her of the girl she'd once been and the woman she wanted to become.

She looked down at the girls, one on each side. They'd snuck into bed for cuddles and had fallen asleep. With Luke lying on the rug beside her bed, all seemed peaceful.

Sarah walked into the grief-counseling session determined to be more open so she could heal faster. She was delighted to see Blake standing and talking with someone by the table holding the coffee machine. She went over to them.

"Hello, gentlemen," she said. "How are you this evening?"

The older man, whose white hair circled his bald head, looked at her with eyes that showed pain.

"This is Bob," said Blake. "I recently bought a car from him. A car for April."

"It was my wife's," Bob explained.

"How nice," Sarah said and turned away when Ellen called the meeting to order.

Once everyone was settled in their chairs and it grew quiet, Ellen began by reading some poetry. When she finished, she said, "Let's go around the room and let each person say whatever they'd like."

When it was Sarah's turn, she said, "I feel as if I've made some healthy changes." She went on to talk about making things as she wanted inside the house and giving away other things she'd never really liked. "I didn't realize how torn I was about keeping things because my husband liked them. Now that I've cleaned house, so to speak, I feel much freer to face a future that doesn't include him except in my memories. And I've begun to write down some things my young daughters might want to know about their father later on. Especially nice times together."

"Excellent idea," said Ellen. "It's interesting that when we are able to move toward a different future, we can do a better job of keeping pleasant memories among others that might not be so."

"Yes, that's what I'm trying to do," said Sarah, proud of herself for being so open.

She listened with the others as Blake told of buying a property to help out a friend and beginning a new life in Lilac Lake.

At the end of the meeting, Ellen came over to Sarah. "I'm pleased to hear you're making wise decisions on your own. I know your parents must be thrilled to have you in town."

"The move here has been a good one. They've been so supportive of me and my girls."

"I'm glad," said Ellen, moving on to another woman.

Sarah left the building, delighted to see stars sparkling in the dark sky. She breathed out a sigh of contentment. Things seemed to be going so well.

She walked, moving briskly in the cool air until she reached Main Street, where her pace slowed as she looked into shop windows to see what was new.

Standing in front of The Wild Flower Boutique, she studied the new items placed in the window and was startled when Poppy suddenly stared out the window at her.

Sarah waved and then waited for Poppy to open the door.

"Come on in. I just got in a skirt and sweater outfit that would look perfect on you."

Chuckling at the way Poppy lured customers to a sale, she stepped inside the store. It was one of her favorites. Poppy had a tasteful eye for merchandise and didn't allow too many items alike, which was nice in a small town.

Poppy led Sarah into the back of the store where she was unpacking some clothing. She held up a chocolate-brown suede skirt and a deep-turquoise, V-neck sweater with tiny flecks of brown in it. "This sweater can be dressed up or down and the skirt is a classy winter look, perfect for a party or something less dressy."

"I love it," gushed Sarah, thinking of Thanksgiving and the upcoming holiday season.

"They're both in your size," said Poppy. "You can take them home and bring them back if you don't like the way they fit. But I'm certain you'll love them."

"Me, too," Sarah said, holding them up in front of a mirror. She turned to Poppy. "Blake told me about the real estate arrangement he's made with you. It sounds like a win-win situation."

Smiling, Poppy said, "It's such a huge relief for me. I couldn't afford to fix up the house. Before he made the offer, Blake told me what changes he had in mind, so I'd be comfortable selling it to him."

"He's a very nice man. His daughter, April, is too."

Poppy's eyes sparkled. "April is lovely. She and I have worked well together in getting her outfits updated. It's been loads of fun."

Sarah paused and then blurted out, "Is anything going on between you and Blake?"

Poppy grinned. "We are seeing where our feelings for one another will take us. We need to be discreet with April and Blake's mother, so we're taking it slow. But Sarah, I've never felt this way about anyone. He's a wonderful man."

Sarah hugged Poppy. "I'm happy for you, Poppy. It seemed as if the two of you clicked right away."

"Yes, that's it. We've talked and talked and have the same ideas and feelings about many things. At my age, I'd given up finding a man."

"Poppy, you're only in your early forties," Sarah protested.

"I know, but while men can choose women of any age, people like me don't have that chance. Less and less with each passing year."

Sarah gave Poppy another squeeze. "I'm glad you found one another. It's going to be lovely if it all works out."

"Thanks," said Poppy. "Let me get these wrapped for you, and then I've got to get going. I'm meeting Blake at my house shortly."

A few minutes later, Sarah left the store with her package. She couldn't stop smiling at the thought of Poppy and Blake together and what it might mean for April.

She arrived home to find her parents and the girls reading together in the living room.

"Thanks for watching the twins," she said, grateful for their help.

"We always love being with them." Her mother gave each girl a kiss and rose from the couch.

Her father hugged the girls and followed Sarah's mother out of the house.

That evening, Sarah fixed herself a cup of hot tea and sat in the living room in front of the gas fire. Taking a deep breath, feeling stronger than ever, she dialed Aaron's number.

When she heard Aaron's deep voice and his sexy hello, a shiver of anticipation swept through her body.

"Hi, Sarah," Aaron said. "It's good to hear from you."

"Thanks. I just wanted to say hello. I'm ready to sow those seeds for that harvest you're always talking about."

He laughed softly. "I'm glad to hear it."

They talked for a while and then one of the girls cried out in her sleep. "Talk to you later," said Sarah, feeling as if she'd made great strides in finding a new pace between them.

CHAPTER FOURTEEN

As the days moved closer to Thanksgiving, Sarah and April worked to get holiday merchandise displayed. Winter snows had yet to come to the town, but those days were not far off. It was a family tradition that the store window was changed the Friday before Thanksgiving, so visitors to Lilac Lake would have the chance to do some Christmas shopping at the store while they were in town.

Mia and Emily were thrilled to be able to be with Sarah as she worked in the evenings after the store had closed to do a few displays. And when it came time to dress the window, the girls played with the fake snow Sarah used and helped spread it around on the floor of the display area. She'd finish without their help.

She'd just climbed into bed that night when the phone rang. *Her mother.*

"Hi, Mom! What's up?"

"It's your father. He's not feeling well. I think he may be having a stroke."

"Have you called Dr. Chambers?" Sarah asked, sitting up.

"Yes, he told me to call 911 and he'd be on his way. But I thought you should know." Her mother's voice shook.

Aware she couldn't leave the girls alone, Sarah said, "I'll get a sitter and be there as soon as I can."

She called Hazel and asked if she'd come to the house.

Hazel sleepily said, "Of course. Give me a couple of minutes to get dressed."

Sarah ended the call and hurried to get herself dressed, her heart pounding with alarm. Her mother would not have called unless it was a true emergency. She was a very strong woman who sounded scared. That worried Sarah most of all.

She met Hazel at the door, gave her a quick rundown of the situation, and said, "I'll call you as soon as I can."

At her parents' house, Sarah saw Emmett Chambers's car and an ambulance in the driveway. Sarah parked in front of the house, got out, and ran to the front door.

Her mother rushed to greet her. "Thank God, you're here. Your dad's worse. They're confirming he's had a stroke. They're preparing to take him to Portsmouth now. We can follow."

Crystal's husband, Dr. Chambers, came over to them. "It's a good thing the EMTs got here so fast. Timing in these situations is so important. I'll follow them to the hospital and make sure everything is right there before returning home."

"Oh, thank you," said Sarah's mother, throwing her arm around Sarah's shoulder and squeezing hard. Sarah knew her mother was as grateful as she that Lilac Lake had a small-town doctor who would give such kind service.

She went over to her dad lying on a gurney and with a nod from one of the EMTs, took hold of his hand and gave it a squeeze. "You'll be all right, Dad. Love you."

Watching him be placed inside the ambulance, Sarah's heart skipped a beat. Her father was much too young to die.

After saying goodbye to her husband, her mother came up beside her. "Are you able to take me now? Are the girls taken care of?"

"Hazel is with them. Let me tell her what's going on, and we'll be on our way. If she can't stay, we'll ask her to get one of the Gilford women to take over for her. I know they will. I don't want you to worry about it."

Minutes later, after confirming with Hazel that she would stay, Sarah and her mother headed to the Portsmouth Hospital.

"How did you know what was going on with Dad?" Sarah asked her mother.

"I recently read an article about the symptoms of stroke. They call it the 'FAST' check. Face, arm, speech and time. Can the person smile? Can the person raise both arms? Can the person speak clearly and understand what you say? If any of these signs fail, call 911."

"Can they tell how bad Dad is?" asked Sarah, fighting tears.

"They'll be able to assess him at the hospital. I'm praying it will be a mild stroke. We're supposed to start our semi-retirement this winter." said her mother, battling tears of her own.

With little traffic on the roads, Sarah made excellent time to the hospital and pulled up to the Emergency Room to let her mother out.

"I'll be right there," said Sarah.

Minutes later, Sarah rushed into the waiting area and found her mother sitting there. "The nurse said they're checking him in now. We're to wait here while they do a number of tests on him."

Sarah sat next to her mother and took hold of her hand. "Hopefully you assessed the symptoms early enough to make a difference. Dad's a strong, active man."

"Yes, maybe too active. I've been trying to get him to slow down. It's been a godsend to have you home helping to run the store. Five months in Florida this winter was going to be the beginning of transitioning the store over to your control."

"That seems so final. I guess it's time to get real about it. I wasn't sure that's what you really wanted."

"If your father survives this and does well enough to continue with our plans, we are going to be making more changes more quickly than we thought," said her mother. Her eyes filled. "I can't lose him or lose the life we've planned."

Sarah handed her mother a tissue. "Dad's in excellent hands, and it's a blessing he was with you when it happened. Hopefully, that saved a lot of time in getting help."

It seemed hours before a nurse came to them. "Mrs. Bullard?"

Sarah's mother stood. "How is my husband?"

"We're waiting for the results from all his tests. Your husband is being taken to a room. We'll be able to give you his room number soon and you'll be able to visit him. He's awake. He's fortunate you called for help right away."

"And the doctor? When can we see him?" asked Sarah.

"He'll meet with you shortly," the nurse said. "We didn't want you to worry."

A short while later, a man wearing green scrubs approached them. "Hello, I'm Dr. Shipman. I'm the one who oversaw your husband's arrival. Lucky man to have someone with him when his stroke happened."

"Can you tell us about his condition?" Sarah asked.

"It appears that he's had a mild Ischemic Stroke which occurs when a blood vessel supplying blood to the brain is obstructed. In his case, it appears that it wasn't for too long, which means a quicker recovery. He's been given a thrombolytic or what we call a "clot-busting" drug to break up blood clots. He'll be prescribed blood thinners going forward. Right now, he's in acceptable shape mentally, and aside from some numbness in his hands and feet, he seems not to have had much damage. We will keep him here in the hospital for the next day or two to make sure there are no reoccurring symptoms."

"Thank you, Doctor," said Sarah's mother.

"Will he see a therapist of some kind?" asked Sarah. "You said he had some numbness."

"Yes, we have a Certified Comprehensive Stroke Center here in Portsmouth. One of two in the state and the only one on the seacoast. We will assign a physical therapist to work with him to see if those symptoms can be reduced. You should be aware that frightening episodes like this can affect people in different ways. He might become depressed, have difficulty expressing or controlling his emotions, become easily agitated. We have staff prepared to help him in this regard, if needed."

After Dr. Shipman left, Sarah went over to the desk to see if her father had been assigned a room, and returned to tell her mother he was on the second floor.

Sarah took hold of her mother's cold hand and knew how tense and upset her mother was. "It's going to be all right. Dad's had a mild stroke. No matter what, it could be worse."

"I know. It's just that I hope it doesn't change his personality like the doctor mentioned. He's always been easy-going."

"One day at a time," said Sarah trying to be encouraging. The thought of her father becoming depressed scared her. She didn't want to go through that experience again.

When they reached her father's room, Sarah followed her mother inside and paused, giving her parents a private moment before she went and hugged him.

Her father was a big, fit man with a jovial personality perfect for selling wares in town. Now, he lay on the bed looking dazed.

Her mother's eyes overflowed with silent tears as she hugged her husband. Sarah felt a sting of tears but thought it best to appear upbeat.

"The doctor says you are a lucky man, that not much damage was done because Mom called for help so quickly." Sarah turned as Dr. Chambers came into the room.

"Hello, Bob. I've been checking on your treatment. Edie is going to be able to have you come home in a day or two. And Sarah, I know you'll be a help."

"Thank you, Emmett," said Sarah. "Thanks for making the trip here."

"Of course. Bob was one of my first patients in town when I was called upon to stitch up a cut finger." Emmett checked his watch. "I'm leaving you in superb care. If anything needs to be coordinated with home treatment, please let me know."

After he left, Sarah walked out of the room to search for some coffee, leaving her mother talking quietly to her father.

Later, while her mother talked to a nurse in the hallway, Sarah gave her father a hug. "How are you, Dad? Are you going to be okay?"

He looked at her with a new uncertainty. “I’m going to do what the doctors and nurses tell me to do. And I’m going to follow your mother’s advice and do some of the recovery in Florida where I won’t have to worry about the store.”

“Yes, Mom has indicated that’s what she wants.” Sarah hid the fact that she didn’t feel ready to take over the store. Somehow, she’d figure everything out. Because she’d do anything to keep her parents happy and healthy.

CHAPTER FIFTEEN

A COUPLE OF DAYS LATER, AFTER THANKING AARON FOR his continued concern, Sarah helped her father enter her parents' house and was thrilled to see that he moved well. A physical therapist had helped him with exercises that made mobility easier. His usual jovial mood, however, was impaired by the constant questions he had about the store.

Sarah felt trapped between her parents' wishes. Her father wanted information and her mother wanted him to stay away from anything to do with the store. After she got her father settled on the couch, she faced both her parents.

"I know you, Dad, are concerned about the business. There's no need. I've talked to the staff, including Wyatt and April, and they're all willing to put more hours into the store for the holiday season. I've also asked Dani Collister to step in to help us. She'll handle a lot of the sales you used to handle. Things pertaining to construction. She's thrilled to help out during this quiet time for her."

"What about the girls? If you're going to be spending more time at the store, who's going to help out with them?" asked her mother.

"I may still rely on you at night," said Sarah. "But GG Wittner found me a babysitter through the assisted living facility. A nice, older woman named Lucille Nordby. She's staying at The Woodlands because her much older husband needed to be there. She, herself, is bored and wants to get out and do something. She's physically able to handle the girls."

"Oh, my! You've been busy," said her mother.

"Yes, I didn't want you to worry about anything. That will get us through the holidays, and then we'll make more permanent arrangements as you prepare to go to Florida," said Sarah.

"What about the financial records?" asked her mother. "I can train someone to take over for me."

"That person would be me," said Sarah. "I know a lot about it but would feel better if you had time to train me thoroughly."

"Sarah, I'm really proud of you," said her father.

"Me, too," added her mother. "It's what we always wanted."

"One step at a time," said Sarah, aware neither of her parents were simply going to walk away from their business. But this time of recovery and subsequent trip to Florida would make it easier on all of them.

Sarah brought the girls over to her parents' house so they could see their PopPop.

Watching them give him hugs and the drawings each had made brought sentimental tears to her eyes. They were very gentle with him as she'd requested.

On the way home, Mia and Emily asked a lot of questions about their grandfather being sick. Sarah kept the details simple but explained that both he and their grandmother would need lots of rest.

Later, back at the house, Sarah overheard Mia and Emily

tell Luke that their PopPop needed lots of rest so he could get better. The girls loved their dog so much and wanted to keep him informed.

Sarah had interviewed Lucille Nordby at the assisted living facility before she introduced her to the girls. But today was the first one where Lucille would pick up Emily and Mia at their preschool, take them home, and watch them until Sarah got home from the store, which closed at six.

Ms. Lucy, as the girls called her, was important to the plans for the store's future. Standing at five foot three, she was a bundle of energy in a well-maintained body that had enough curves to appear comforting. Her hair was dyed blond and went well with her fair coloring and still youthful face.

Anxious to see how the afternoon went, Sarah left the store in a hurry.

Luke met her at the door wagging his tail, and as she patted him, she inhaled a delicious aroma of something cooking. Chicken perhaps.

Lucy walked out of the kitchen. "I hope you don't mind. Mia said she was hungry, and I thought I'd surprise you with dinner."

"Oh, thank you so much!" cried Sarah, giving her a hug. "I dreaded the thought of having to prepare it."

Laughing, Lucy said, "The food at The Woodlands is very good, but I like to mess around in the kitchen. It's something I've missed doing since my husband and I came to the assisted living facility. Unfortunately, he's living in the special memory care area for Alzheimer's patients while I have my own room in the main building. It was the best compromise I could think of. But it has its drawbacks."

"You'll eat with us, won't you?" said Sarah taking in deep breaths to inhale the smell of the dinner.

"I'd like that," said Lucy, taking off an apron Sarah had tucked in a drawer and never worn.

"Where are the girls?" asked Sarah.

"In their rooms. I gave them each a board book to read," said Lucy.

"How nice," said Sarah. "Let me get them, and we'll eat right away, unless you want to take the time for a glass of wine."

"A glass of wine sounds lovely," said Lucy. She held up a finger. "But I promise you I'd never drink on the job. It's only because I'm with you that I'm doing it now."

"Understood. I'll say hello to the girls and then pour us each a glass. This calls for a celebration."

Lucy laughed. "I'll set my place at the table."

Sarah returned to the kitchen, poured two glasses of pinot grigio, and led Lucy into the living room, where they sat on the couch facing the fire Sarah had turned on in the fireplace.

"How did you do with the girls today? Were they ready to go home with you? Any trouble?"

Lucy shook her head. "They're lovely children. And so interesting. They really do seem to know what the other is thinking."

"They get along well, with only a few squabbles natural for siblings," said Sarah. "I work very hard to call them by name and treat them the way they want to be treated. Mia is more outgoing, but Emily knows what she wants."

"Yes, I can see that," said Lucy.

"Do you want to extend your duties to making dinner

three nights a week? I think five would be too many, don't you?"

"Yes," said Lucy. "We've only discussed my working for you during the week. Now, with your parents thinking of leaving for Florida after the holidays, we could talk about the weekends. I have a friend who might be willing to share weekends with me."

"Another woman at The Woodlands?" Sarah asked.

"Yes. She and I go to our gym class together. She misses her grandchildren and would like to earn a little money for extras."

"Write down her information, and I will do a background check on her."

"It's so endearing that Genie Witner wanted to make sure I'd do a good job for you," said Lucy. "I guess that's how it works in a small town."

"Lilac Lake is a very special place," said Sarah.

After Lucy left, Sarah drew a bath for the girls and spent some time talking to them about their day.

"How do you like Ms. Lucy?" she asked.

"She's nice," said Emily. "She gave us books."

"And she read to us," Mia said. "Now we know how to read them."

Sarah chuckled. Mia loved memorizing words.

"Ms. Lucy will be picking you up from school every day. She may even help out over the weekends. We'll have to see. Would you like that?"

Both girls smiled, and a small part of Sarah relaxed. She wanted to get as much organized at the store as possible before her parents left town.

A few days later, her mother called. “I know you like to meet your friends at Jake’s on Saturdays. I need a break. How about my babysitting the girls at your house so you can join them?”

“That would be wonderful,” said Sarah, delighted. “I haven’t seen my friends in a while.”

“Why don’t you count on me to babysit for Saturday evenings and for your grief counseling meetings? I’ve missed my girls.”

“How is it going, Mom?” Sarah asked. “I know Dad needs to have quiet, restful times as well as his physical therapy. But has his attitude changed?”

“A little,” her mother admitted. “He’s used to being in the middle of things. This recovery time is difficult for him because he feels well even though there is still some numbness in his feet. It makes him more cautious. And his patience is worn thin at times.”

“My daytime babysitter, Lucy, is terrific. I’ll try to stop by and visit Dad more often, keep him updated on the store,” said Sarah.

“That would be very helpful, dear. Oops! Gotta go! Your father is calling me.”

Sarah ended the call and sat a moment thinking of her parents. Even though they were struggling a bit, they remained optimistic about the future. That’s what had been taken away from her after Jesse’s suicide.

CHAPTER SIXTEEN

THURSDAY, THANKSGIVING MORNING, SARAH PREPARED the turkey she'd ordered several weeks ago from a local farmer and slid it into the oven. Crystal had called earlier that week to say she was preparing extra side dishes and desserts for Sarah and her family. Sarah gratefully accepted her offer. Crystal was the former owner of the Lilac Café and was an excellent cook.

Her mother and father would come for the meal but wouldn't stay long because this first week after his stroke was important for her father. He was to rest as much as possible when he wasn't working on his physical therapy exercises. The chances for a second stroke were still there, even though his had been a mild one.

Still, Sarah wanted the girls to have all the fun of drawing pictures for each of them, to be placed on their chairs at the dining room table. Because Sarah would be working all day on Friday, she was allowing the girls to set out some of the Christmas decorations they loved.

By the time her parents were due to arrive for dinner, the place was a chaotic mess, but Sarah didn't care. It was nice to have a bit of Christmas in the house after an awful scare with her father. Besides, it kept the girls busy while Sarah researched Millie Harriman, Lucy's friend at The Woodlands. She'd already called to wish GG a Happy Thanksgiving and had been given a kind word about Millie. Still, she liked to check online to see if there were any hidden tidbits good or bad about the woman. Satisfied that there were no issues with Millie, Sarah decided she'd go to see her over the weekend.

"Happy Thanksgiving!" the girls cried when her parents entered the house.

"Remember to be gentle," Sarah told them softly before they ran to her mother and father.

"Hi, PopPop, are you resting?" Mia asked.

Sarah's father grinned. "I'm supposed to rest. But I'm glad I'm here. Something smells delicious."

"It's the turkey," said Emily. "It's big."

"It's a special one," said Sarah. "And Crystal has made side dishes and one of her famous pecan pies for dessert."

"I'm so glad she did that. I brought my pumpkin pie but that was all the time I had," said Sarah's mother. "I've been setting up the books for next year so you wouldn't have to do that. We'll meet a little bit each day next week to go over things. And this week, I'll help out with the girls while you hold a couple of his and her Christmas shopping events at the store."

"Excellent," said Sarah, glancing at the look of disappointment on her father's face. "Don't worry, Dad, I'll fill you in on the activities."

Satisfied, her father relaxed.

Sarah led her parents to the table and while the girls explained the pictures they'd made for them, Sarah carried the turkey into the room to show them.

"We have so much to be thankful for," said Sarah's mother. "And this is a beauty."

Sarah took the turkey back to the kitchen to carve it.

Her mother came to help her carry the side dishes into the dining room and wrapped an arm around Sarah. "Thank you, darling, for making this so nice."

"Like you said, we have a lot to be thankful for," said Sarah, realizing how much she meant it on many different levels.

Once the food was on the table, Sarah said, "Today, both girls get to say grace."

Emily went first. "Thank you for this food. It's my favorite."

Mia said, "My turn. Thank you for the turkey and pie."

"And I'm sure we're thankful for the vegetables and PopPop's healthy recovery," said Sarah's mother.

"Amen," said Sarah and her father together, amused.

"Let's eat," said Sarah's father.

With mouthwatering anticipation, they all dug into the food. From a distance, Luke watched them.

Later, after the girls were tucked into bed, Sarah went through the boxes of decorations, setting aside those for a tree. Aaron had mentioned taking the girls to cut down a fresh Christmas pine on a nearby farm. She hoped that was something he was able to do.

She walked through the house, placing the decorations the girls had played with. A couple of decorations, sad reminders of Jesse, she put in a box to be given away. After straightening and storing the empty boxes, she climbed into bed. Tomorrow was a big shopping day at the store.

The next morning, a few people were already waiting when Sarah went to unlock the front door of the store.

After greeting her customers, Sarah went about lighting up the place, making mental notes of things to be done, displays to be tweaked, items to be ordered. Wyatt and April had worked together to display holiday and home items in various locations as well as in the special Christmas shopping area she'd set up next to the front window. She'd learned the more convenient an item was to buy, the better the chance it would be sold. The store now had several spots holding irresistible items, both practical and for pure fun.

She'd also learned she couldn't sell what she didn't have. Many items that were sold needed to be replaced by back stock or quickly reordered. It was almost a game, keeping things stocked in the store without overdoing it.

Dani walked into the store carrying a cup of coffee for her. "Thought you could use this to start the day. It's going to be a long one."

"Thanks," said Sarah. "You have no idea how much I appreciate your help."

"It's fun for me. I'm comfortable answering questions about construction or home improvements. Truthfully, I've been thinking of finding something to do when I'm not needed at The Meadows construction site. I'm available for consulting jobs. I've done a few out of town. But I want something steadier, close to home. Especially because we're hoping to start a family."

"After the holidays are over, perhaps we can talk more about it."

Sarah loved having Dani at the store, where she didn't need much training and had already taken the initiative to list an order in construction supplies.

She started upstairs to her office and turned back. "If

Blake Loomis comes into the store, please have him come see me. I want to work out a plan with him to buy all his supplies from us at a discount. My father has done that for other people in town. It's a win-win situation.

"Will do."

Sarah went to her office to go over the financials of the week. The more she thought about Dani working at the store on a permanent basis, the more she liked it. Who knew what was going to evolve from her father's stroke?

Saturday evening, Sarah closed the store right on time, excited to think of having some time with her friends. It meant the world to her that she had people around who supported her. And she was anxious to see Aaron. He'd called to check on her, of course, but she needed to see him in person to know how things really stood between them.

She drove into her driveway, saw her mother's car there, and let out a sigh of relief. Lucy had worked the morning shift and her mother had spent the afternoon with the girls. It was a test of how a schedule might be going forward with Lucy's friend.

Inside, the girls greeted her and then went back to the coloring books they were working on. Sarah turned to her mother. "Thanks for taking care of them. How did you like Lucy?"

"She's lovely and fun," her mother said. "You're lucky to have her. She told me she has a friend who's willing to babysit."

"I'm still trying to decide about staff assignments at the store. Are you ready to show me what work you do at the office?"

"I think so. I wanted these first days at home for your father to be easy. But I think I'll have more time to spend with you."

"Thanks. I'm going to take a shower and get ready for tonight." Sarah gave her mother a hug. "I feel like I'm in high school about to go to a dance."

Her mother laughed. "It's nice to see you like this. Go, get ready to have some fun."

A few minutes later, Sarah stood in the shower letting the warm water sluice over her, loosening muscles tightened by a busy day. After having the twins, she'd worked hard to get back in shape, but she'd soon realized her body would be forever changed. She didn't mind. It was more important to be healthy. And happy. And she adored the girls.

She decided to wear the new slacks and sweater outfit she'd bought from Poppy's store. She wanted to feel special tonight because she hoped to have a chance to spend some time alone with Aaron. She wanted to make clear to him that her becoming busier at the store didn't mean any less interest in moving forward with him.

When it was time to leave, Sarah kissed the girls and promised them a lazy morning the next day. The store didn't open until noon, and she intended to have some special time with them before Lucy came for the rest of the day.

When she walked into Jake's, several people waved to her from the locals' tables in the corner. Her gaze settled on Aaron, and he stood holding out the empty chair next to him.

She approached and greeted everyone before sitting next to Aaron, loving how he'd put his arm around her. She ached to turn into his embrace and kiss him but held herself back. He'd let her know when he was ready for that kind of display in front of others.

Several people asked about her father.

"He seems to be doing fine. He's frustrated he can't do more, especially at this busy time of year. But my mother is making sure he follows the doctor's instructions."

"Someone in my family, an uncle, had a stroke," said Tessa. "He was getting better, then he had another stroke. That time, he didn't make it."

Sarah could only stare at her, feeling as if she'd been slapped.

"Tessa, why do you do that?" asked Misty. "You make everything about you, and it's always so depressing."

"I'm just trying to be part of the group. So, maybe it wasn't an uncle, maybe it was a relative of a friend. It doesn't matter," said Tessa, tossing her shoulder in dismissal.

"It wasn't helpful," said Sarah quietly. "Everyone knows how worried I am about my father recovering."

Whitney spoke up. "Dani and Brad are on their way. She's loving helping at the store, Sarah."

"She's such a wonderful addition," said Sarah. "Has everyone ordered?" She needed to talk about anything else but her family and the store.

Damon left the bar and came over to them to say hello and take orders.

After Sarah ordered a small bowl of clam chowder and a salad, Aaron turned to her. "We need to talk about a Christmas tree."

"Yes, you mentioned an outing with the girls. We'd love it."

"I can come too," said Tessa, leaning across the table to face them. "It seems like such a New Hampshire thing, cutting down your own Christmas tree."

"This is a family thing for Sarah and her girls," said Aaron quietly, apparently annoyed by the intrusion.

Dani and Brad arrived and nothing more was said about Tessa going with Sarah and Aaron. Still, Sarah felt uncomfortable with Tessa's obvious attraction to Aaron.

After spending a few hours with the group, Sarah was more than ready to leave when Aaron quietly asked if he could spend some time alone with her.

She climbed into his truck so they could sit and talk.

Behind the wheel, Aaron pushed back the seat and faced her. "You look beautiful tonight."

"Thank you. It's been a hectic several days, but I'm glad to have this chance to be out of the house and to be able to spend some time with you."

They stared at one another for a moment and then Aaron reached over and cupped her face in his hands. Then, keeping his gaze on her, he lowered his lips to hers.

Sarah closed her eyes, savoring the wave of heat racing through her body.

When he pulled away, Aaron smiled at her. Then his lips met hers for a deeper, longer kiss. All the worries of the last few days grew smaller. If she had Aaron's love, she could manage the challenges she'd been given. Tears of relief stung her eyes.

Aaron ended the kiss and rubbed her back. "How are things, really?"

"They're a bit hectic, but lots of pieces are falling into place. I told you I was going to hire Lucy to help with the girls.

She's turned out to be a true gem. She has a friend who's willing to exchange places with her on weekends and perhaps other times. My main concern is seeing that Mia and Emily are taken care of. Dani and a couple of high school kids have stepped in to help the regular staff at the store. I'll be training with my mother to go over the financial work she normally does. I'm pretty sure I can hire out some of that."

Aaron studied her thoughtfully. "Sounds like you have things covered. How about you? Have you had time to deal with your personal issues?"

Though he asked her in a soft gentle tone, Sarah knew how important her answer was.

"Next week will be my last time at grief counseling. I needed a new perspective on things, and I'm comfortable with my emotions. The group is there if I need a few reminders. But I've taken steps of my own to help me be able to move on."

Aaron gave her a steady look. "Then, I'm ready to start dating you. Is that what you want? It's not like I'm asking you to the prom. This is serious on my part."

"On mine too," said Sarah. "And though it isn't wise for you to spend every night with the girls and me, I want to make sure that we can be together."

Grinning, Aaron tugged her closer. "I want to make sure of that too."

Sarah's eyes filled at the tender way he was gazing at her. She'd been so foolish to think she'd have a better life away from Lilac Lake and him.

He wrapped his arms around her, and she leaned up against him, never wanting to leave.

CHAPTER SEVENTEEN

Sunday afternoon, Lucy arrived at the house with her friend, Millie Harriman. Millie was tall and thin with gray hair cut short in a bob that suited her sharp features. But her eyes, a pretty green, held such warmth that Sarah was immediately put at ease.

She called to the girls to come greet the women.

They dashed into the front hall and stopped.

Lucy said, "Mia and Emily, I'd like you to meet a friend of mine, Ms. Millie. She's going to help me take care of you from time to time. I told her you were wonderful girls. I hope you show her how truly special you are."

Wide-eyed, the girls said, "Hello," together.

"Oh, my! That hello sounded musical to my ears," said Millie. She lifted a harmonica out of her purse. "I bet we can have some fun together."

Sarah grinned at the two older ladies. "You didn't tell me there would be music. That's terrific."

"We'll see how it goes," said Lucy. "Millie and I have a lot of things to share with Mia and Emily. It should be fun."

"I won't be gone long. The store closes at five. Enjoy yourselves. The girls and I made cookies for you." She kissed the girls and said, "Okay, now you can have more cookies."

"C'mon," said Mia, tugging on Lucy's arm.

Emily and Millie followed them into the kitchen.

Before any trouble could begin, Sarah called out, "Goodbye," and left the house.

At the store, she spent some time rearranging items, doing a quick look, and making a list of things to order tomorrow. Dani, who'd opened the store, stood by as Sarah told her what she was doing and why. Display was such a big part of marketing. It was something Sarah loved to do.

Sarah took advantage of this quiet time to talk to Dani about running the store, the changes she'd made since coming to town, and what she envisioned for the future.

Dani listened and made some suggestions of her own.

Sarah realized it was too soon to ask, but she had to know. "Would you be interested in having part of the business? I haven't spoken to my parents yet, but it might be beneficial to all of us."

"Do you mean buy into the business?" asked Dani, surprised.

"Maybe," Sarah said. "I might be thinking too far ahead. But now that Aaron and I are seriously dating and you're trying for a family, it might be right for me to have another partner going forward. Think about it. I don't want to mention it to my parents unless I know it's of interest to you."

"Wow! It's something I hadn't thought about. Bullard's Hardware Store has been a part of Lilac Lake since I was girl coming here. How would your parents feel about having an outsider in the business?"

"I'm not sure," Sarah said honestly. "But your family has been part of Lilac Lake longer than mine, so you aren't exactly an outsider."

"I'll talk it over with Brad and get back to you. But initially, I'm excited about the idea," said Dani, giving Sarah a hug.

"Wonderful. It's something to think about. That's all it is at this point," said Sarah.

"Agreed. In the meantime, a mob of people are headed to the store." Dani hurried behind the cash register, while Sarah went to usher them inside.

The days were busy with the added time commitment to learn more about what her mother did to help run the store behind the scenes.

April and Wyatt turned out to be a compatible team working together. They were taking care of receiving the shipments, entering items into the computer system, and tagging the merchandise.

One afternoon, Sarah brought them into her office to discuss their procedures.

"I'm very pleased to see how hard you're both working, dedicated to getting the job done, even staying late some days. I know how important it is to have some extra cash at the holidays, and you'll find a bonus in your paycheck this week."

April and Wyatt smiled at one another.

"Thank you, Ms. Miller," said April. "I appreciate it."

"Yes, me, too," said Wyatt.

"You're welcome. Keep up the good work. That will be all," said Sarah.

As April and Wyatt left her office, a young female approached them. It took Sarah a moment to realize it was Lindsay Legget, Wyatt's girlfriend.

"Hi, Lindsay," said Wyatt. "What are you doing here? This is a private area."

"You promised to meet me at the library," Lindsay told Wyatt. "Instead, I find you here working with ... with April Loomis of all people. What's going on with that?"

Wyatt made a face. "You know perfectly well I work here. April does too. We work together."

"I don't like it. You're spending more time with April than you are with me."

"It's a job, Lindsay. That's all it is," said Wyatt.

Sarah watched something like disappointment flash across April's face and disappear and realized that April really cared for Wyatt.

She got up from her chair and went to speak to Wyatt and Lindsay. "Is there a problem here?" Sarah asked, studying the tall, thin blonde who'd teased April at school to the point of downright bullying.

"I'm just talking to Wyatt," said Lindsay in a dismissive way that irritated Sarah.

"Wyatt is at work. I suggest you converse with him when he's not doing his job. How did you get up here? There's a sign marked 'private' clearly posted at the bottom of the stairway."

"I knew Wyatt was up here," said Lindsay, stepping back as Sarah continued to approach them.

"I'll walk you downstairs," said Sarah. "We don't want to interrupt the work Wyatt and April are doing."

"I'll call you later," Lindsay said to Wyatt. "You'd better answer."

Wyatt gave me a look of embarrassment and turned away without responding to Lindsay.

At the bottom of the stairway, Sarah spoke quietly to

Lindsay. "Don't come back to the office area again. Like you said, you can always phone Wyatt."

Sarah watched Lindsay walk away, head and shoulders high. She knew high school was tough for a lot of kids. People like Lindsay, so entitled, so mean, made it even worse for some like April who was sweet-natured. She didn't know the Legget family. They were among the newer residents.

Sarah went back to work and decided not to say anything about it to either Wyatt or April.

Sarah freshened up after work to attend her last group grief counseling meeting. Being with other people who were dealing with loss had helped ground her. Talking about Jesse to a non-judgmental, sympathetic group of relative strangers had put her feelings in better perspective, allowed her to cope with a lot of her anger, disappointment, and guilt.

As part of the process, she was eager to thank the friends she'd made in the group for their help.

Her mother was staying with the girls and gave her a big hug as she left. "I'm really proud of you, Sarah, for dealing with this issue. It was a wise idea to repeat the counseling you had earlier. You've grown a lot."

"Thanks, Mom," said Sarah, letting out a long breath. "I needed this. Aaron and I knew we had to wait to date exclusively until it felt right. Now, we have a chance to start over with one another. I've always loved him."

"I know. This time it seems right."

Sarah studied her mother, seeing how much she cared. She hoped to be as supportive to her daughters as they went through the ups and downs of life.

###

Sarah walked into the meeting room carrying a plate of cookies the girls and Lucy had baked. It was a tradition that when someone in the group felt ready to stop attending, they would treat others as a farewell gesture.

Seeing her, Blake grinned and walked over to her. "I'm glad for your progress. I need to stay for more meetings, but this group is terrific about encouraging people to leave when they're ready."

Sarah asked him, "How are things with you and Poppy?"

"Okay. She moved into Misty's cabin this past weekend, as you may know. Now that the sale of the house has gone through, I'll begin work on the renovations. I figure I can take my time. I'll still be living with April and my mother while the work is being done on the house. I'm going to move my mother into The Woodlands sometime soon. It'll be easier for all of us, especially April."

"I'm glad to hear it. She's a lovely girl." Sarah debated whether to tell him about Lindsay confronting Wyatt about April but decided not to interfere.

At the end of the meeting, Sarah shared a few hugs with a couple of people she felt close to and left the building glad she'd realized she needed to deal with her grief and guilt. She knew the ordeal wasn't over, but she was on the right path.

As planned, Aaron met her outside the meeting. She rushed to him and threw her arms around him. This relationship is what she'd been fighting for.

On Sunday, while Dani handled the store, Sarah took the day off. Aaron was coming to pick her and the girls up to go get a Christmas tree. The girls were old enough to count down each day until Christmas, marking off the days on the special Christmas calendars Sarah's mother had given them. Now that they were getting a tree, their excitement grew.

Wilson's Tree Farm was an institution in the area, a convenient place to find and cut your own tree. It was a festive place with Christmas music and a roadside stand that served hot cocoa and coffee by helpers dressed up with Santa hats. Much to the girls' delight, a big spruce growing near the stand was decorated with colorful lights that blinked off and on,

Aaron parked his truck, and they headed out.

Each year, different sections of the tree farm were opened up for cutting. Though the area had had some light snow, the ground was clear and hard, making the trek into the woods easy. The girls raced ahead as Aaron and Sarah walked hand in hand behind them. Aaron carried a chain saw and Sarah held onto an empty wagon to haul the tree back to the stand to be trimmed and paid for.

The girls raced from one tree to another, declaring each one was the best.

"Okay, Mia and Emily, you can choose between this tree or that one," said Sarah, making it a simpler choice. "Which one do you want?"

After much guessing back and forth, they chose the smaller tree Sarah wanted, and Aaron went to work cutting it down.

They loaded the tree onto the wagon and tied it down, then hurried out of the cold back to the stand for hot drinks.

This ritual was such a simple thing, but Sarah knew the girls would remember it always. All the way home, they chatted, describing every detail.

###

Later, after Aaron had put the tree in a stand and placed all the lights on it, the decorating began. Though she liked it to look pretty, Sarah decided she'd let the girls place the ornaments where they wanted. If later, they needed to be moved around, she'd do it after they were in bed.

"Will you place the star on the top of the tree?" Sarah asked Aaron.

"Sure. Who's going to help me?" he asked the girls.

Patiently, he lifted one girl and then another to make sure the star was just right.

Watching him, tears stung Sarah's eyes at how sweet, how gentle Aaron was with her daughters.

When she and Aaron collapsed on the couch, Mia crept into Aaron's lap and Emily climbed into Sarah's. Luke lay at their feet. This scene seemed so right.

Later, waiting for dinner to be cooked, the girls played in their room while Sarah and Aaron sat in the kitchen enjoying a glass of wine.

"Thank you for all you've done for the girls and me," said Sarah, clicking her glass against his. "You've made it very special for all of us."

"I enjoyed it," said Aaron. "This time of year always makes me remember my mother. I think she'd be pleased for me to be with you and the girls."

"Did you celebrate the holidays in the same way as a child?" Sarah asked.

Aaron shook his head. "For one thing, we never cut down our Christmas trees, but decorated a living one for birds and other animals. Remember, I grew up poor in things, but rich in blessings, even after the Collister family took me in."

Sarah went to him and wrapped her arms around him. "That's why we, who know you, are so lucky to have you in our lives. You make us better people."

Aaron drew her closer before giving her a long, deep kiss that left her reeling.

"You're kissing!" came a cry beside them.

"Are you Mommy's boyfriend?' asked Emily, standing by her sister looking up at them.

"Aaron is special to all of us. Right?" asked Sarah, pulling herself together the best she could.

Mia and Emily nodded solemnly.

"Okay, we're about ready to eat. You may set the table."

Sarah put placemats, napkins, and silverware on the table. "Remember how?"

"Yes," said Mia. She took the placemats and set one in front of each chair. Emily followed, placing a paper napkin in the center of them. Together, they figured out where the silverware went.

Sarah oversaw them, proud of the way they worked it out between them. She'd vowed to begin early to teach the girls some basic living habits.

After Aaron and the girls were seated, Sarah dished up the meal—baked chicken with a creamy sauce, peas, and mashed potatoes on each plate.

"Remember, no complaining about the food. You must have at least a bite of the peas," said Sarah.

Aaron looked on without commenting, but Sarah saw approval in his eyes. Having her daughters be part of the equation of getting back together with him was a challenge not many young men would agree to take on.

They finished the meal in relative quiet, and then Sarah instructed the girls to get ready for a bath.

As Sarah stood at the sink rinsing dishes, she felt Aaron come up behind her and sighed happily when he nibbled on her neck. She turned around and nestled against him. After feeling so alone, so unsettled for such a long time, she filled with contentment.

"Thanks for dinner," he said, kissing the top of her head. "Sorry, but I have to go."

She looked up at him. "Thanks for a great day. It was special for so many reasons. I wish you could stay."

"Me, too," said Aaron, "but ask me again, and I'll arrange things so I can say yes."

"That's a deal," said Sarah, accepting another kiss before he pulled away.

Later, after the girls were in bed and asleep, Sarah wondered what it would be like if the day came when it was right for Aaron to spend the night. She could hardly wait.

CHAPTER EIGHTEEN

With the Ye Olde Christmas Faire going on in Lilac Lake, things became even busier for Sarah and the store. One afternoon, after her mother had shown her the financials for the month, Sarah said, "Mom, we need to talk honestly."

"Yes, I think so too," said her mother sitting back in her desk chair.

"We need to think about the future, not just this winter but going forward," said Sarah. "You and Dad are going to be away like you planned. And I'm pleased for you. But I need more help at the store when you're gone and beyond."

"I agree. I've been wondering what we can do about it," said her mother. "Dad and I are pretty well able to retire. We've bought and paid for a condo in Florida, our home here is paid off, and we have a nice retirement savings program. All those years of hard work are finally paying off."

"After Dad's stroke, I think you two should be able to relax and enjoy life. I've always known you wanted me to take over the business, and I'm pleased to do it. But I want to be able to have my own life and time with the girls."

"Absolutely," said her mother.

"That's why I'd like to bring in Dani Collister as a part owner. She can handle the hardware section of the store while I continue to do the house and garden and gift sections and oversee all the stock. We'll keep our staff. We can hire a bookkeeper, and you and Dad can review the monthly statements with me. Does that sound reasonable?"

"Yes, it does. Dad is anxious to get back into the store, but I've told him he can't work until after our stay in Florida. He'd already promised me that."

"I hope that being able to play golf and do some of the other things he enjoys will help him make the change more tolerable," Sarah offered. "I don't want him to think I'm chasing him out. I'm just trying to be reasonable about the reality of my running the store."

"You're absolutely right. It is important, however, that he can always feel he's still part of the business, even if it's only looking over daily or monthly reports. We can't ask him simply to walk away," said her mother.

"What about you, Mom?" Sarah asked. "Is it going to be hard to make this change?"

"Not really. I'm going to have more time with the girls, get back into quilting, and, believe it or not, I've promised your father I'll learn to play golf."

"Okay, you and Dad talk about this and come back to me with any thoughts you have, and we'll approach Dani, who's already said she's interested. Even though I have children and she and Brad are trying for some, we both are dedicated businesswomen who can help one another out and do an outstanding job for all of us."

Her mother sighed and turned to Sarah. "It's another life change, but it's a good one. And during the summer and fall, when we're staying here, we'll still be able to step in occasionally and help with the girls and the store." She rose and gave Sarah a hug. "We're so lucky to have you for a daughter."

"Thanks," said Sarah. "I feel lucky too."

Later, at the close of day, Sarah locked the front door and walked through the empty store making sure all was in order before slipping out of the back and getting into her car to go home.

Sarah used the week's Christmas Faire to display and sell gifts she'd selected months earlier. It was gratifying to see that she'd chosen well. Holiday sales were an important component of annual income. New shipments were coming in daily, and Sarah was glad to see how well April was doing entering items into the computer program. Wyatt kept up with the task of stocking items upstairs or restocking things throughout the store. He already was reporting to her the things he'd noticed she might want to reorder.

In addition, they had six full-time sales employees who were excellent at not just ringing up orders, but selling to their customers, many of whom they'd known for years.

On the fourth day of Ye Old Christmas Faire, Sarah's local social group planned to gather at Jake's. Every store and restaurant had been kept busy, and it was a chance to relax temporarily because the next day they'd be busy all over again.

After making sure Mia and Emily were happily settled with her mother, Sarah left for the restaurant. She and Aaron had talked on the phone, and she was looking forward to seeing him. When she walked into Jake's, the place was crowded with Faire visitors filling the bar area and the cocktail tables. Sarah wended her way through them and was delighted to see many of her crowd sitting at the two tables reserved for the locals.

She was especially glad to see Dani and Brad there. Dani was excited to become part of the store business, but Sarah hadn't had a chance to speak to Brad. She slid into a chair beside him and spoke quietly, "I'm thrilled to have Dani on the team. I hope you are too."

"Yes," Brad replied. "It puts Dani's knowledge of architecture and construction to use and will give her the flexibility she wants. I'm sure she'll have some ideas to add to what you already do."

Sarah chuckled. "I'm sure." Though the store had been in business for years, it was time to grow and change it a bit.

When she saw Aaron walk over to them, Sarah lifted her purse from the chair next to her and waved him over.

He slid into the seat, wrapped his arm around her, and hugged her. "How's the tree holding up?"

Sarah laughed. "It won't have one needle left by the time Christmas is over." She'd told him earlier how the girls liked to change the ornaments around, almost like a game. Their constant fussing was taking a toll on the tree, but Sarah saw how much creative fun they were having and let them continue.

The group was a congenial one, and they laughed over things that had happened with various visitors.

Dani told the story about a well-dressed woman who came into the store looking for a toilet plunger. She was a guest at the Lilac Lake Inn and didn't want anyone to know it was needed. "I had to wrap it up like a gift so she could take it back to the Inn," said Dani, chuckling.

Poppy spoke up. "I had a customer who insisted she could

wear a dress that was too tight on her. In the end, I convinced her it must have been mislabeled and she needed the next size up, which was also mislabeled."

"Did she buy the bigger one?" Dani asked.

"Yes," said Poppy. "But I had to remove the size tag inside."

Laughing with the others, Sarah realized she hadn't been this happy in a long time.

Aaron turned to her. "You and the girls are coming to the Collister's Christmas Party with me, aren't you?"

"Yes," Sarah said. "My parents will be with the girls and me Christmas morning, so we're able to come that afternoon. Thanks for inviting us."

"Mary Lou would be disappointed if I hadn't." Aaron grinned. "She's been able to figure me out since I first came to live with them. And she knows how I feel about you."

"I'm excited to go. I haven't told them yet, but I know the girls will be too."

"The house will be crowded with people and kids. But it will make a big difference to me to have you there."

"And I'm looking forward to having you at my house for Christmas Eve. The girls will be wild with excitement, but hopefully we can get them to bed at a decent time."

"I hope so." Aaron's dark gaze focused on her, and she felt a shiver of anticipation shoot through her.

"Hey, you two! What are you doing for New Year's Eve?" asked Tessa. "I thought I might throw a party for everyone."

"We have plans," said Aaron, surprising Sarah.

"Oh, okay. I guess I'll have to come up with another idea. Everyone's busy but me."

"Won't you be busy at the inn that night?" asked Sarah.

"Yes, but I'm talking late-night party," said Tessa. "Never mind. It was a bad idea."

Sarah felt a little sorry for Tessa, but she didn't want to ruin any plans Aaron might have for her. She knew from the way Aaron had flexed his jaw that he didn't care for Tessa. She also knew there must be a very strong reason for him to feel that way.

After their drinks and dinners had been eaten and the dishes cleared by the wait staff, people began to leave.

"Ready to go?" Aaron asked her.

"Sure," said Sarah. "Want to come to my house for a while? It's early yet, and the girls should be in bed."

"Okay," Aaron said, walking her to the door. "I'll meet you there."

Sarah got in her car and drove to her house, full of excitement. She and Aaron hadn't spent too much alone time together. And now that she was ready to move their relationship forward, she wanted that time with him.

At home, Sarah thanked her mother for staying with the girls and ushered her out the door. She went to check on the girls and was delighted to see that they were both sound asleep.

Aaron arrived just as Sarah turned on the fireplace and then, for the first time that evening, they fully embraced and kissed.

"You feel good," said Aaron, rubbing her back up and down as he leaned in for another kiss.

Sarah had always thought the phrase "she melted in his arms" was an exaggeration, but she now understood it was a perfect description for how she felt. They'd hugged and kissed as high school kids, but this was so much better. For Sarah, the feel, touch, and smell of him was both familiar and new.

When they pulled apart, Sarah said, "Do you want something to drink? Wine? Water? Coffee?"

"Water sounds fine," said Aaron.

"Get comfortable in the living room and I'll bring it to you," Sarah said.

A few minutes later, she entered the living room and saw Aaron stretched out on the couch.

She brought the water to him, set it down on the end table, and sat beside him on edge of the couch.

"It's nice seeing you here like this," Sarah said. "It seems right."

"Yeah, I feel the same way. We've taken a detour, but it feels right to be back together again." He gently tugged on her arm, and she lay down beside him.

Nestled against him, Sarah lifted her face, and Aaron's lips came down on hers. She felt a tremor go through her and realized how long it had been since she'd felt such a strong sense of need ripping its way through her. She wanted whatever he was ready to give.

A while later, Sarah got up off the couch and went to get a blanket to cover Aaron. As a construction worker, he worked as many long, hard hours as daylight would give him. She'd forgotten that. When she returned to him, he smiled and tugged her down beside him. They lay cuddled together on the couch. They didn't speak. Words weren't necessary. Sarah believed Aaron loved her as much as she loved him. The day would come when they'd tell one another. But, for now, she was content to begin the journey of being together like this.

CHAPTER NINETEEN

CHRISTMAS EVE FESTIVITIES AT SARAH'S HOUSE ALWAYS began a little late because there were usually last-minute shoppers at the store who needed to be catered to. No one was more anxious than Sarah to close up and go home to the girls. Her parents normally came for a dinner of Chinese takeout but had opted out this year. Instead, they were coming to tuck the girls in bed for the night and then leaving so Sarah and Aaron could have some time alone.

Her mother greeted Sarah at the door when she got home. "Merry Christmas Eve!"

"Thanks," said Sarah giving her mother a kiss. "See you a little later."

"Enjoy the evening," said her mother. "Dad and I will be back soon. He's resting before the big reading event." Tucking the girls in bed on Christmas Eve was a ritual everyone loved, especially her father. He'd read them special Christmas stories in their bedroom before turning out the light and leaving the door ajar in case Santa needed to peek inside to make sure Mia and Emily were sound asleep.

She turned as a knock came at the door. "This must be Aaron now."

When Sarah opened the door, Aaron stood there holding a sack of Christmas presents and a big bag from the Won Ton restaurant. Wearing a Santa hat, he looked adorable. Emily and Mia looked on wide-eyed and mouths agape.

"Perfect," said Sarah. "Come on in. Mom's here, but she'll leave and return with my father."

"Merry Christmas, Mrs. Bullard," Aaron said.

"And to you," her mother said cheerfully. "But, please call me Edie."

"Thank you, Edie ," Aaron replied with a big smile and then moved toward the kitchen.

Sarah's mother gave her a wide smile. "He's so nice. I'm glad he's back in your life, Sarah."

"Me, too," said Sarah, knowing their growing relationship was the best gift anyone could have.

She showed her mother out and returned to the kitchen. Aaron had set the food down on the counter and was stacking his gifts on the kitchen table.

"I thought you and the girls could open my gifts tonight, if that's all right with you." He turned to her and wrapped his arms around her before lowering his lips to hers.

When they pulled apart, the girls were climbing into their kitchen booster seats.

"Presents!" cried Mia.

"Are they for us?" Emily asked.

"Yes, they're from Aaron. We're going to open them after we eat. But, if you want, you can open the cards he's giving you while I serve dinner."

She turned to Aaron. "What would you like to drink? A beer?"

"Yes, thanks," he replied, sitting at the table so he could tell the girls about the Native creatures drawn on the cards.

The girls listened intently as he told about the loon who was sometimes called a "spirit bird" who took messages to the

Abenaki god.

Overhearing him, Sarah was elated that he wanted to share a bit of his heritage with them.

She served the girls plain chicken pieces, rice, and some carrots.

"Okay, come help yourself, Aaron. We've got a lot to choose from."

By the time Aaron was done, Sarah was chuckling at the amount of food on his plate. That was something she'd have to keep in mind going forward.

Aaron kept the girls' attention with stories of his own Christmas celebrations as a young boy.

"Maybe next year we can feed the birds," said Emily.

"I think that's a lovely idea," Sarah said.

After the meal was over, Sarah said, "Why don't you girls take your gifts from Aaron into the living room. You can open them there." She looked at Aaron. "If you don't mind, I'll open your gift to me later when we're alone. I have one for you too."

The girls were still playing with the stuffed animals Aaron had given them when Sarah's parents walked inside.

"Look what I got," said Mia running to them with a stuffed raccoon. "He plays funny tricks on people."

"And I got a turtle who helped the world," said Emily importantly.

"What thoughtful gifts," said Sarah's mother smiling at Aaron as he rose from the floor to greet them.

Aaron shook hands with Sarah's mother and then with her father. "Glad to see you looking well and up and about."

"Thanks. It's been a wake-up call for me. We'll do our

story book routine and then go home." He glanced at Edie. "Maybe I could have one beer?"

"Maybe a cup of tea," said her mother pleasantly but firmly.

"I'll get that for you," said Sarah. "Mom, can you help the girls into their pajamas? I'll see that they have baths tomorrow before we go to the Collister's party."

Left alone in the living room, the two men took seats on the couch. Sarah could hear them talking about sports, and after a pause, she heard Aaron tell her father that he was serious about her.

"I don't play games," said Aaron.

"I've always liked you, son," said Bob. "Glad to see you two together."

Sarah clutched her hands prayer-like. She hadn't realized she wanted her parents' blessing on this newest change in her life.

And later when her parents had gone and the girls were asleep, when she and Aaron sat on the couch staring into the flickering fire and relaxing, Sarah was even more grateful that she had a new family dynamic.

"I want you to open my present now," Aaron said. He went to the kitchen and returned to her with a small, square package wrapped in something that looked like birch bark but was handmade paper, as he explained.

She removed the red ribbon and lifted the top off the box. Inside, resting on a creamy silk fabric, a gold necklace held a delicate sunburst with a stunning turquoise center.

"It's lovely," Sarah gushed.

"The sunburst is for happiness. And the turquoise is thought to be a protective gem. I thought it was perfect for you," said Aaron, a bit shyly.

"Here, help me put it on," said Sarah.

"It's small enough to wear every day," said Aaron, hooking the chain behind her neck. "That's why I got it. So, it wouldn't be just for a special occasion, but would remind you of me all the time."

"It's gorgeous. I love it and the feelings behind it," said Sarah. She patted the necklace against her skin just above her heart. "Now, it's time for me to give you your present." She got up and reached behind the Christmas tree, where she'd placed his rather large present.

She placed it on the floor in front of him on the couch. "I hope you like it. I thought it had a special meaning for you."

Aaron's eyes lit with excitement. He ripped the paper off and lifted the carved wooden bird. "It's awesome. The detail on the loon is beautiful."

Sarah kissed him. "I know the loon has a place in Abenaki history. Just like the toy you gave Emily."

"Yes, when the loon calls out, they are reporting news to Gluskabe," said Aaron, rubbing his palm over the wood. He reached over and pulled her to him. "Thank you. It's a very special present. And means a lot more coming from you."

"Tell me about Gluskabe," said Sarah. "I know he's a central figure in many of the Abenaki legends."

"He's kind and helpful and teaches us about our culture and about the Great Spirit, who is the source of all life. He has magical powers and can turn monsters into harmless animals. That's what makes this gift to me so special. The loon can spread the news to Gluskabe about us."

Satisfaction filled her. She kissed him and when he deepened the kiss, she knew he, not a thing, was the best present she could ever receive.

They cuddled and talked in soft whispers so as not to awaken the girls.

"I want you to come to my cabin," said Aaron. "Soon."

"How about New Year's Eve? I'm sure I can get my mother or Lucy to stay with the girls."

"Perfect. I'm planning on having a house built at The Meadows someday. In the meantime, my cabin serves me well."

"I remember going there in high school. Has it changed much?" she asked.

"You'll see. It's a lot more comfortable. I've added onto to it."

"Well, then, I can't wait to go. Why don't we have the Lilac Lake Café put together a special meal for us? They've been advertising New Year's Eve specials."

"Sounds delicious," said Aaron. "I keep the kitchen well stocked, but I don't have any fancy foods."

Though she was still waiting for him to say those three special words to her, Sarah stared at Aaron's dark eyes. They told her how he felt about her. She could hardly wait for New Year's Eve.

CHAPTER TWENTY

CHRISTMAS MORNING WAS HECTIC WITH THE GIRLS OPENING gifts and playing with them while still another gift waited to be opened.

Her mother and father sat in the living room watching them, delighted to be part of such excitement. On a quieter note, Sarah gave gifts she'd selected for her parents with Florida in mind. Most of them were geared toward playing golf.

As she watched her parents open them, she realized, as her mother had once said, that they all were beginning a whole new phase of their lives. It was both sad and exhilarating.

Sarah offered more coffee and food while the girls played with their new toys, and she sat with her parents in the kitchen.

"Your new necklace from Aaron is lovely," her mother said. "It's very tasteful." She smiled at Sarah. "I'm really proud of all you've done for yourself in the past several months. The girls are content and have acclimated to life here in Lilac Lake. It's a great place to raise children."

"We're thankful to have you here," said her father. "After the holidays, we'll work on getting things settled in the business so we're all satisfied with it."

"When are you driving to Florida?" Sarah asked.

"I see the doctor on the 12th of January and then we want to leave by the 15th," said her father.

"That should give us enough time to put things in place," said Sarah, wondering if this sense of loss is how her parents had felt before she headed off to college.

"By the way, Aaron didn't ask for my blessing, but he assured me how serious he is about you," Sarah's father said to her. "It was a man-to-man gesture that I liked."

"He's that kind of person," said Sarah, unable to hold back a sense of pride.

"The girls speak of him with affection," said her mother. "You won't do anything crazy with him while we're away, will you?"

"By crazy, do you mean eloping?" asked Sarah, intrigued by the thought.

"That or anything else that leaves your father and me out of it," said her mother. "We had a few reservations with your wedding to Jesse, but we're really excited about the chance for you and Aaron to be together."

"Deal," Sarah said, though her mind was spinning. *She didn't recall any hesitancy about her marrying Jesse. Not really. Well, maybe. She'd just known she didn't want to go back to Lilac Lake. Not yet, anyway.*

The girls came into the kitchen.

"We want juice," said Mia.

"Do I hear a please?" said Sarah. She got to her feet. It would soon be time to put them down for a "rest" before the party at the Collister's.

That afternoon, when Sarah pulled up in front of the Collister's farmhouse, she parked in the lot near their fruit and vegetable stand and took hold of each girl's hand.

"You're going to meet a lot of people," Sarah told them. "I want you to be polite and kind."

"Okay," said Emily. "Will Aaron be there?"

"Yes. This is his family. He'll help introduce you," Sarah said, looking up to see him waiting on the front porch for them. "There he is now."

Both girls dashed ahead to greet him.

"Glad you're here," said Aaron when she reached him. "Everyone is waiting to see you. I should warn you that I've never invited a woman to the Christmas party before. There will be questions."

They kissed, and then Sarah straightened. "I'm ready."

As soon as they walked inside the house, Mary Lou Collister hurried over to them. "Hi, Sarah. It's so nice to see you here. It's a very special occasion for us." She gave Aaron a meaningful look.

"Thank you. It's nice of you to invite me and the girls." Sarah was amused by the way Aaron was shuffling his feet like an embarrassed teen.

"Aaron, will you please help introduce Mia and Emily? Sarah and I are going to have some time alone."

Mary Lou took Sarah's elbow and led her into what was a small room holding a lot of craft materials. "I didn't want to embarrass you in front of everyone, but I need to know that this time you really are serious about Aaron. I've never seen him happier than he is now. I don't want that to change."

Somewhat taken aback, Sarah studied her. "I know how much you love Aaron. I promise not to hurt him. We're seeing where our relationship goes."

"Aaron would be furious at me for quizzing you, but he is

my special child, the one who was given to us." She glanced at the turquoise sunburst necklace Sarah wore.

Sarah stood there uncertain whether she should say something or simply leave. Before she could decide, Mary Lou wrapped her arms around her.

"We'll welcome you into our family with open arms. I've known you for years, and you're a beautiful woman, inside and out. And those daughters of yours are adorable. I hope the day comes when you all will be part of the family. In the meantime, forgive my being so protective and enjoy the party."

Sarah returned the hug Mary Lou gave her. "Thank you."

"If there's anything I can do to help you two, just let me know."

"Thanks," Sarah said again, touched by how protective Mary Lou was of Aaron. She knew Aaron adored her, and now she knew why.

"You go ahead," said Mary Lou. "I'll follow in a few minutes." She took a tissue out of her pants pocket and dabbed at her eyes.

When Sarah entered the living room, Aaron came right over to her. "There you are. I wondered where you'd gone and then figured Mama Bear was doing her thing. It's all part of a ritual she goes through when one of the kids is serious about a possible spouse."

"Where are the girls?"

"They're in the playroom, playing with cousins. Five of them are about the same age."

"That will keep them busy," said Sarah, chuckling.

Joe Collister came over to them. "Welcome, Sarah. Glad to see you here. Has this guy brought you a drink?" He gave Aaron a questioning look.

"What'll you have? Wine or punch?" Aaron asked her.

"Wine, please," Sarah said.

When Aaron moved away, Joe said, "I hope Mary Lou didn't scare you. She always wants to make sure things are right, and she adores Aaron."

"Yes, she told me. It's sweet."

"Glad you see it that way," said Joe.

They both looked down as a small pig ambled toward them wearing a big red bow.

"Ah, have you met Pansy yet?" asked Joe.

Sarah laughed. "I've seen her at the vegetable stand a few times. She looks very festive."

Aaron returned and handed her a glass of wine. "C'mon, Sarah. I want you to meet some of the family from out-of-town."

As Sarah followed Aaron, she glanced at Dani, who was talking to a woman holding a baby. Sarah recognized the woman as one of Brad's sisters. Seeing the expression of longing on Dani's face, Sarah's heart went out to her.

Aaron led her to a pleasant-looking couple. "This is one of the family's favorite cousins from Durham, Rick Collister and his wife, Susan. They have two boys Mia and Emily's ages. They aren't twins. Just close together."

"And we have an older child, a daughter who is seven, Gaby," said Susan. "The family is growing rapidly. My sister is here somewhere. She's pregnant with twins. You might be able to give her some insight. I met your girls earlier. They're adorable."

"Thanks," said Sarah. "What do you do in Durham?" Sarah asked her.

"Rick is a professor at UNH, and I teach at a preschool," said Susan. "We keep very busy. I understand you own Bullard's Hardware Store. Dani was telling me she's working there for a while."

"Yes," said Sarah. "She's been taking over for my dad who's been ill. I'm hoping to bring her on board on a permanent basis."

Susan lowered her voice. "Poor thing hasn't been able to get pregnant. I'm hoping that changes for her and Brad."

"Me, too," said Sarah.

Aaron ended his conversation with Rick, and he led Sarah around the room introducing her to other family members. It was a congenial group, and when it was announced that dinner was ready, they all cooperated in a buffet line in the kitchen while Mary Lou and Aaron's sisters made sure the tables were kept supplied with lots of delicious food.

A table for the children was set up in the playroom and two of the adults sat with them to make sure all went well. Sitting beside Aaron at the dining room table, Sarah was very aware of how welcoming his family was. Being with them at this older age, Sarah appreciated it more than ever.

When it came time to take the girls home, Aaron helped her strap them into their booster seats.

"I'll follow you home," said Aaron.

"Thanks. The girls are like rag dolls after such an exciting day," said Sarah. "Your parents are so generous to give them each a doll."

"You know what Mary Lou is like. She loves being able to do it," said Aaron. "See you soon."

CHAPTER TWENTY-ONE

SARAH AWOKE THE NEXT MORNING AND REACHED FOR Aaron. He'd stayed long enough to make sure she was tucked into bed properly, according to him. Thinking of what that had meant, she smiled to herself.

She rolled over and checked the clock and wished she didn't have to go to work at the store. But the day after Christmas was usually a profitable business day for them with people willing to spend Christmas money on a few extras. She'd put Wyatt and April to work retagging items for their annual January sale. Upstairs, she'd be starting to put together data for year-end reports.

"Mommy, Mia won't let me play with her doll," cried Emily storming into her bedroom.

"You have a doll of your own to play with," said Sarah, holding out her arm and pulling Emily in for a snuggle. "We're all tired from the excitement of Christmas. Just relax and enjoy the day with Lucy."

"Maybe Lucy will read to us. She makes sounds like all the animals," said Emily.

Mia came into the room. "Okay, Emily, you can play with my doll." She climbed up into bed and snuggled on the other side of Sarah.

Lying there, surrounded by her children, Sarah thought back to last night with Aaron. She wished he'd been able to spend the entire night, but it wasn't time to do that yet.

After giving the girls breakfast, Sarah got ready for work. She and Dani were going to set up things so that a year-end inventory could be done right after the New Year. In the meantime, Sarah was going to try to clear out as many holiday items on sale as she could.

When she got to the store, there were a few people waiting at the door for the after-Christmas sale. Sarah had already posted on a sign on the door stating that Christmas Items would be 40 percent off.

She parked out back, went through the store turning on lights, and then walked to the front door and opened it. She knew most of the faces and admired how some people in town used the post-Christmas sales to build their holiday décor at home.

Dani arrived with coffee for them both. While Dani oversaw the cash register downstairs, Sarah climbed the stairs to her office. She looked over the sales lists from before Christmas and had an idea of what had sold. The rest of the Christmas items would be assembled in one location with a sign 40 % off, and Dani and the other staff people would be encouraged to try and sell those items.

April and Wyatt arrived within minutes of one another, and Sarah set them to work moving things around and remarking price tags.

Throughout the day, working on financials, checking to see how sales were going, stepping in to help at the cash register, Sarah realized how important it was for Dani to be part of the operation.

When the store closed at six o'clock, Sarah asked Dani to stay. She pulled a bottle of white wine out of the refrigerator in the staff kitchen and said, "Let's sit and talk for a minute, if you have the time."

As they sipped the wine, Sarah laid out her idea for a partnership role for Dani and then sat back.

"Tell me what you think. My parents are open to having you own part of the store and, heaven knows, we need you. We have reliable staff and can hire more, if necessary, but with the kind of store it is, we need to have owners on hand to check on daily reconciliations, inventory needs, and oversight of the store and its displays."

"Brad and I have discussed it," said Dani. "Our concern is that we need to have time together. The store is open seven days a week, but I'd certainly need days off. Brad is busy with his construction business and works late whenever the weather permits. But I need flexibility to be with him."

"Exactly," said Sarah. "I need someone who is flexible not only for me, but so they have time off when she needs it."

"You know we're trying for a baby," said Dani, her eyes becoming shiny with held back tears.

"Yes, I know. And when that time comes, we'll adjust our schedules. I trust you, Dani, and respect your knowledge of the business. That's why this is important to me."

"And if I get a big consulting job?" said Dani.

"That, too, is something we'll deal with. I just don't want the responsibility of the store alone. In the summer months, Mom and Dad will be around to help, but we'd still be in charge of the store for the sake of consistency."

"Okay, I love the idea of going in with you on the store," said Dani, lifting her glass of wine and clicking it against

Sarah's. "Thank you so much for thinking of me. There's only so much work I can do at The Meadows helping clients design their new houses. Besides, I wanted to pull away a bit in order to have something of my own going on."

"I would think that would be important for any relationship," said Sarah.

"Absolutely," said Dani. "I love Brad like crazy, but I need some space in order to make my life with him even better."

Sarah tucked that piece of information in her mind. She knew how important space for oneself was. When Jesse was feeling low, he'd stayed at home bringing everyone down.

They hugged, and Sarah left the store feeling better about the future. As she'd told Dani, if necessary, they'd hire more people.

The next few days were busy taking care of sales and making notes of missing inventories in the smaller sections of the store. After the New Year, she and Dani, Wyatt, and April, would close the store on a Sunday to complete the inventory.

The girls were a bit restless away from preschool. Sarah's appreciation for Lucy and Millie grew. Taking care of the girls was a nice break for the older women and a valuable help to her.

When her mother suggested Sarah take an extra day away with Aaron at the cabin for New Year's Eve, Sarah jumped at the chance to tell Aaron. He was delighted.

Sarah dropped everything and hurried to Poppy's store to buy a glittery dark green sweater she'd seen earlier, hoping it was still there. It would be a perfect addition to the casual slacks and jeans she usually wore.

Poppy was helping a customer when Sarah walked into the store. She raced over to the table where she'd seen the sweater. It was gone.

Poppy looked up at her. "Are you looking for the green sweater you liked?"

"Yes, but it's not here," said Sarah.

"I saved it for you. I had a feeling you might want it when I heard you were going to Aaron's cabin for New Year's Eve," said Poppy.

Sarah laughed. Living in a small town was both delightful and a little frightening when everyone knew your business.

The customer left, and Sarah looked over other sale items. "How is the renovation of your old house was going?"

"Better than I thought," said Poppy. "Blake has taken out a few walls already, but he tells me that's just the beginning. I'm thrilled about it. The house has been in the family for years."

"And how are things going with you and Blake?" Sarah asked, aware she was playing into the small town gossip circle.

A pretty pink blush covered Poppy's cheeks. "Very well. We've clicked from the beginning, and it's getting better and better. I think it was a matter of timing for both of us. And now we're ready to build a healthy, lasting relationship."

"Oh, Poppy! That's wonderful," said Sarah, giving her a big hug. It sounded as if they, too, were building a love to harvest. It was a concept she loved.

Sarah left the store, raced home to put her things away, and returned to the hardware store, excited for her holiday retreat.

CHAPTER TWENTY-TWO

On the morning that she was to leave for Aaron's cabin, Sarah packed the girl's clothes and special toys in matching overnight bags and waited for her mother to pick them up. When her parents left for Florida, it would be a sad day for her and her girls. But it was only right that they had time to relax and play in the sun after years of hard work at the store.

Still, when her mother entered the house to get the girls, Sarah felt a pang of worry about how she'd handle everything. She kissed Mia and Emily, gave her mother a hug of appreciation, and held onto Luke's collar as they left the house. Luke didn't know it, but he was about to have a fantastic time roaming in woods with two playmates.

Alone in the house, Sarah quickly straightened it and then took her time packing. It would be for only three nights, but she wanted to be sure to pack correctly. She hadn't been to Aaron's cabin, the one he'd bought in high school with money he'd earned working with Brad, and he'd made a lot of changes since then. She heard it was beautiful.

Finally, she loaded her suitcase, grocery bags, and Luke into her car and took off. She'd had a few dismal New Year's Eve celebrations these last few years and was now ready for something different with a man she was in love with, not that she'd told him with those three special words.

Sarah drove around the near end of the lake and up the side of it across from the Lilac Lake Inn. David Graham's parents had a house right on the lake. The Graham nursery acreage climbed the hill next to Aaron's land.

She turned into the gravel driveway of Aaron's house and made her way up to where a lovely log cabin style home sat. Sarah stared at it with disbelief. In high school, Aaron's cabin had been tiny and not very sophisticated. This home was gorgeous with large windows overlooking a sweeping front porch and the woods beyond it.

As she got out of the car, she turned and could see a streak of blue in the distance and realized it was the lake. Such a stunning view.

Aaron came out the front door of the cabin and walked down to her car, followed by his two black Labs. "Welcome to the cabin!"

He put his arms around her and lowered his lips to hers in a welcoming kiss that sent tingles through her body.

When he pulled away, he smiled at her. "Better let Luke out of the car."

"Oh, yes," said Sarah suddenly aware of the noises the dogs were making. She opened the car door and watched Luke jump out. Tail wagging, he greeted the other dogs before sprinting away.

"Let him go. He'll be safe in the woods," said Aaron. "Let me help you carry your things inside. There's a little bit of snow on the ground, but more is coming."

Sarah let Aaron carry the bulk of her heavy things while she followed with bags of groceries and special treats.

Aaron set down the suitcases inside the door. "I have a guest room upstairs or you can sleep with me." He gave her a sexy look and waited for her answer.

"I want to be with you," Sarah said, feeling her cheeks go hot.

"Good," said Aaron. "That's what I want, too. I'll carry the suitcases in there. Why don't we put the food in the kitchen and then follow me."

Aaron took a couple of the food bags from her and led her through a living room with a huge river stone fireplace to a modern kitchen with warm cherry cabinets and rich green counter tops. She set the bags on a center island and gazed around.

"This is gorgeous. And, you have every convenience I can think of," she said, noting the warming oven, the indoor grill, and the two dishwashers.

"I decided if I was going to make this cabin larger, I would protect the investment by making it a dream home for any interested buyer and enjoy it for myself."

"Okay, you'd better show me more. I'm in love with it already," Sarah said.

"Follow me to the master suite," he said. They walked through a dining area of the open living space and into a hallway that led past a half bath, a laundry and into a large room that contained a massive king-size bed, facing a television screen above a built in fireplace. On either side of the fireplace French doors led to an outside patio that housed a sizeable spa.

She followed Aaron past a dressing room with a huge walk-in closet into a bathroom with two separate sinks, a soaking spa tub and a shower for two.

"Wow! You've thought of everything. Who wouldn't love all of this?"

A look of pride crossed Aaron's face. "We sometimes give prospective customers a tour of the place to show them what we can do at The Meadows or any place they choose. As Dani would point out, it's the finishing details that help make it special."

"Every bit of it is beautiful," said Sarah. "I love my little cabin, but this is way beyond that."

A look of pride crossed Aaron's face. "Upstairs, there are three bedrooms and two baths. Again, it's a house suitable for many people. That was the whole idea." He grinned. "Let's see what you treats you brought."

Sarah laughed. Aaron was well-built and not the least bit fat, and he loved to eat.

They passed through the dining area into the kitchen. That's when Sarah noticed the covered wooden deck outside the kitchen. "Oh, you have an outdoor kitchen. That's another bonus."

"Yes. I think we put in everything people might want. There's an attached three-car garage and a small barn out back for the tractor and other garden items. In the summer, there are plenty of wildflowers growing. David Graham did some landscaping for me, but I want it to be as natural as possible.

"Well, anyone would be thrilled to live here if you ever decide to sell it," said Sarah. "Aren't you going to build a house in The Meadows?"

"I have the land, but I'm not sure what I'm going to do," said Aaron, peeking into one of the grocery bags and lifting out a bag of cookies. "Chocolate chip. Great choice."

She laughed. "Go ahead and have one. I brought the fixings for sandwiches for later."

They put away the food and the bottles of wine she'd brought to celebrate with.

"Thanks for doing all this," said Aaron. "I have some food to share with you, too. But now that you've seen the house, I want to take you on a walk through my land. Ready to go?"

Sarah looked down at her sneakers. "Should I put on my hiking boots?"

"Yes, he said. "You'll be more comfortable. And you'll need gloves and a hat in addition to your jacket. It's pretty cold out there."

"Okay, hold on. I'll get ready." Sarah hurried into the master bedroom and over to the smaller closet where she'd hung a few things and grabbed the hiking boots she'd brought with her. She put on a pair of wool socks and pulled on the boots glad she'd thought of them.

Aaron was standing by the back door. "The dogs are waiting for us outside."

The moment Sarah stepped outdoors, the cool air captured her breath. She laughed when Luke dashed over to her, his tongue hanging from his mouth stretched into what only could be called a doggy smile.

She patted him on the head and watched as he ran away.

"Knight, Coal, come!" ordered Aaron, and the two dogs hurried to him. "I want them to know that you're with me. Go ahead and pet them."

As they sat at attention, Sarah rubbed their ears and quietly talked to them. They were beautiful dogs and very obedient.

Aaron clapped his hands. "Okay, go!"

They galloped away.

Aaron led her to the wooden barn-like structure. "This is

where I keep my utility tractor. It's supposed to snow heavily tonight. I'll attach a small plow to it and keep the area around the house cleared of snow. Maybe make a few paths so we can walk in the snow."

"That sounds very... romantic," said Sarah noticing the smile that was creeping across Aaron's face.

He took hold of her hand. "I want to show you my Maple grove. It's very special. Come spring, I'll tap the trees for sap to be boiled down into maple syrup. The process is something that reminds me of my mother and how she loved to tell stories about the beauty of the trees allowing us to use them for something sweet." He chuckled. "She did that to keep me helping her with the sugaring."

"You've had such an interesting childhood," said Sarah. "I love how you're keeping some of the traditions relevant today."

They continued to work through the woods until they came to a spot that looked as if the trees had been planted in a grove.

"In the fall, the colors here are special. Now the bare trees look as if they're waiting for the sap to run again."

"Winters in New Hampshire can seem long," said Sarah. "I love having something to do when it's not quite winter or spring but somewhere in between." She pointed. "What's that building? It looks like some sort of shed."

"It's my sugar house, where I boil the sap. You'll notice the building is louvered at the top to vent the steam from the boiling sap."

"Tell me more. I'm interested, and I think the girls would be, too," said Sarah.

"The sap is gathered in buckets and brought here to be

cooked down. The sap must be boiled the same day it's gathered, so a hot and steady fire is kept going at all times during the processing. You must boil the sap to between 180 and 200 degrees before canning it in jars or bottles. Then it's stored for up to two years on a shelf."

"How long have you been doing this?" asked Sarah, impressed by what he'd told her.

"I started after you left for college. I needed something to help keep me busy," Aaron said quietly.

"I know you have your syrup in some places nearby," asked Sarah. "We could put some in the giftware section of my store."

"I sell it to Beth Beckman for her shop at Beckman Lumber but I'm sure she wouldn't mind if I sold you a small amount too. I don't make enough syrup to make a big business out of it."

"I'll ask Beth about it," said Sarah. "I don't want any hard feelings."

Aaron checked his watch. "Are you hungry? I'm grilling steaks for dinner, but I could use a bite to eat for a late lunch."

"Sounds good to me," said Sarah. Her cheeks were stinging a bit from the cold breeze that had picked up since they'd been gone.

It took a while to make it back to the house, but Sarah didn't mind being next to Aaron, listening to him talk about plans for expanding the residential development he and Brad Collister owned.

"We want to keep the neighborhood like it is. It's a high-end market, but that allows us to build a product that is in sync with the natural habitat around each house. People who've already bought there want to keep the same atmosphere."

"Absolutely. You don't want to ruin it by getting greedy about money," said Sarah.

"Yes, that's it," said Aaron with a hint of admiration in his voice.

Inside the house, they hung up their outerwear and took off their boots. Then while Sarah made sandwiches, Aaron turned on the gas fireplace, which Aaron explained was fueled by the propane gas tank sunk into the ground.

"What about the stack of wood I saw by the barn?' asked Sarah.

"That's chopped and ready for the sugar shack," he said walking into the kitchen.

Sarah handed him a plate. "Here's your sandwich. Ham and Swiss on Rye. Right?"

He grinned. "You got it."

They sat on bar stools at the kitchen island eating when the gray skies that had followed them into the woods opened up, sending snowflakes hurrying to the ground.

"Looks like it's going to hit pretty hard. The forecast said 5 to 6 inches, but I sometimes get more up here," said Aaron.

"It makes me feel cozy inside," said Sarah putting their dishes in the farmer's sink.

Aaron came over to her and wrapped his arms around her. "I can make you very cozy by the fire, and no one will interrupt us."

She looked up at him and saw the glimmer in his eyes.

A bolt of longing went through her.

"Yes," said Sarah. "I'd like that."

As they walked to the fireplace, Sarah saw that Aaron had

already placed a soft Indian design blanket on top of the large blue Oriental rug in front of the fire.

A large, long brown leather sofa sat farther back on the rug giving them space to maneuver.

They sat on the blanket and then lay down on it, face to face.

Staring into Aaron's dark eyes, Sarah saw love there. Gentleness and shyness too. She knew no matter what happened between them she'd remember this moment because she could sense its importance.

She'd known from the way Aaron had invited her to his cabin that it meant more than a casual visit. And she wanted it to be that way. To have a few days with him alone to see if what she'd always imagined about living with him was true.

They'd grown apart and now were together again. This time with him was deeper because of their earlier separation and what each had gone through.

Aaron caressed her hair and tucked a strand of it behind her ear. "All the better to see you," he murmured. "I thought you were hot in high school, but you're beautiful now. Motherhood has made it so."

"You've seen me, Aaron. I show those scars," she began ...

Aaron stopped her with a kiss.

She met his passion with her own, and when he helped her remove her top and sweater, he was as excited as she.

Soon they were naked on the blanket.

The twilight darkened the skies outside, and the fire flickered, sending light on his sharp, strong features. His eyes swept her body and he murmured, "Beautiful," before he took her in his arms.

###

Later, sitting in front of the fire sipping wine, Sarah felt contentment she'd never known fill her. Aaron was a generous lover with few demands. He didn't need them. It was as if they'd always been lovers, knew how to give one another pleasure.

Even now, just relaxing next to him, Sarah knew she was loved and protected. It was such a different feeling from what she'd gone through with Jesse's last years that she silently whispered thank you to whoever might hear.

"You hungry?' Aaron asked, rubbing her back. "I'm ready for dinner. I'm grilling a steak. Mary Lou sent over her famous Collister potato casserole, and David Graham's mother baked us an apple pie."

Sarah's eyes widened and she couldn't hold back a chuckle. "Do you always get food provided to you?"

He gave her a sheepish look. "They like to do it. It makes them feel needed, and though I can cook, things like that are always appreciated."

Laughing, she hugged him. "You're so spoiled." She loved that other people were drawn to Aaron. He was such a kind, thoughtful man.

They got up and headed to the kitchen. Sarah heard movement behind her and realized the three dogs were hungry too.

While Sarah fed the dogs, Aaron opened a bottle of merlot.

"This is a terrific red wine," said Aaron, handing her a glass of it. "I think you'll like it."

She accepted the glass from him and clinked it against

his. "Here's to a happy, healthy New Year!"

"Yes," said Aaron, settling his gaze on her. "I'm glad you're here. It means a lot."

"To me, too," she said. "It's already been fantastic."

He winked at her, sending a warm wave of happiness through her.

As they sipped their wine and talked, they worked together to get dinner on the table. Because of the growing storm outside, Aaron decided to pan fry the beef filets and add a garlic herb butter sauce. That, scalloped potatoes, and a green salad which Sarah put together made a scrumptious meal.

When they finished, Sarah said, "I don't think I have room for dessert. Do you want to save it for later or even for breakfast?"

"Breakfast? I like that idea," said Aaron. "Leave the dishes."

"No," said Sarah. "I like to leave the kitchen clean after a meal. I've learned it's better that way."

Surprised, Aaron said, "Okay, I'll help."

Such simple words, but to Sarah they meant everything. As Jesse grew worse, he wanted nothing to do with helping in the house or with the girls. She recalled how she'd begged him to go to the doctor to adjust his medications. But he thought it was a sign of weakness and didn't like how the drugs made him feel.

Tears suddenly stung her eyes. She turned away so Aaron wouldn't see.

"Hey, what's up?" Aaron asked, coming up behind her and wrapping his arms around her.

"Just a bad memory," she said. "I'm having such a lovely

time here that it hit hard."

"C'mon, let's go see that movie you wanted to see," said Aaron.

"While you get it ready, I'll finish here." She looked out the window at the snow falling at a steady pace. "Good thing we're well supplied. It looks pretty bad out there."

"I don't know about you, but I like snowstorms. It's great being in the woods, listening to the quiet and connecting all over again to nature."

Sarah faced him. "I love that about you. You see beauty where others don't."

He smiled. "I'll go put on that movie."

CHAPTER TWENTY-THREE

As interesting as the movie was, Sarah felt her eyelids closing. She couldn't remember having such a feeling of peace. She didn't have to worry about the girls. Luke was lying in front of the fire with Knight and Coal. And the store was closed for the holiday.

She felt rather than saw Aaron lift her off the couch and carry her to his bed. She stirred enough to take off her clothes and then climbed into the bed beneath the fluffy, warm duvet he kept there.

Sometime in the night, she awoke. When she realized where she was, she rolled over to find Aaron curled beside her. It was deliciously surprising, as if he'd appeared from one of her dreams of him.

She got out of bed to go to the bathroom and hurried back to the nest they'd made beneath the duvet. Aaron stirred enough to reach for her but then went back to sleep.

In the early morning, Sarah got up, found her bathrobe, and padded into the kitchen, leaving Aaron in bed.

She made coffee in the kitchen and stood looking out the window at the snow that had piled onto the ground. She, too, loved the peaceful quiet following a snowstorm, the way the white snow covered so much, like frosting on a cake.

She heard Aaron come into the room and turned to find

him in his pajama bottoms smiling at her.

"The princess awakens," he said, walking over to her and giving her a hug.

She laughed. "Thanks for taking care of me last night. The food, being outdoors, everything here combined to make it impossible for me to stay awake."

"This air has that effect on some people," he said. "I'm going to grab some coffee and then go out and clear the driveway and other areas in case we get more snow. I've discovered it's best to be prepared."

"Sounds like a plan. I'm going to soak in the tub and hopefully do some reading." She let Luke and the other two dogs outside. They were big enough to romp in the six or more inches of snow before being called to come back inside.

"Enjoy yourself," said Aaron. "It will be another day of relaxation. I know you don't have many."

She kissed him. "Thanks."

Later, lying in the tub, she thought about the possibility of living here one day. She'd inspected the bedrooms upstairs and could envision the girls settled in two of them. It would be healthy for them to have their own space.

Sarah hadn't realized Aaron lived in such luxury. He'd kept it quiet. And in all the time they'd been seeing one another, he'd never invited her to come see it. She supposed this time together was a greater test than she'd thought.

She got out of the tub, dried off and dressed in jeans and a cozy sweater. She'd save the sparkly green sweater for tonight's New Year's celebration. She brushed her hair, put on some makeup and sprayed a bit of her favorite perfume on her wrists and behind her ears.

When she walked into the living room, she saw that Aaron had started a fire in the fireplace. She called to him but when she heard the rumble of the tractor plowing snow outside, she realized that's where he was.

She went to the window to check on him. With his long dark hair tied back, she could see the happiness on his face. He loved being outdoors.

She took the book she'd brought with her and went to the couch. Reading was a true luxury for her, and she intended to make use of the time she had here to enjoy it.

After a while, Aaron came inside. "It's beautiful out there. Come see." She set down her book and went to him.

"Get your snow gear and hiking boots. I want to teach you to snowshoe."

Outside, light snow was falling, flakes floating down from the sky, making Sarah think of the snow globes the girls had received for Christmas.

She stuck her tongue out to catch a few and then picked a clear space to lie down to make a snow angel.

Laughing, Aaron threw himself down on top of her. "M-m-m, I like snow angels. A certain one in particular."

As he kissed her, all three dogs hurried over and nosed them playfully. "Go away!" he cried, pushing at them, which made them more excited.

"Crap. Let me help you up," Aaron said to her. He pulled her to her feet and hugged her. "Let's try snowshoes."

Moments later, Sarah walked on the trail Aaron had made in the woods. It took a sort of rhythm to use the devices. But she could see how much easier it was to walk.

After a while, Aaron said, "I'm ready to go inside. I bet you are too."

She laughed. "More than ready. I'm using muscles I didn't know I had."

"That's why I don't want to have you overdo it today. It's supposed to be nice tomorrow and I want to take you on a hike."

As they were taking off the snowshoes on the back deck, Sarah looked out at the garage and barn. "I had no idea you owned so much land and that your cabin was really a gorgeous home."

"I like to keep my retreat private, except when it's used for business."

The dogs came inside with them and rushed over to the fireplace hearth to warm up.

"What can I get you for lunch?" Sarah asked. "Would you like another sandwich? Or maybe some clam chowder I bought from the Lilac Lake Café."

"The chowder sounds delicious," said Aaron, taking off his jacket and hanging it on a hook in the back hallway.

"What do you want to do for the rest of the afternoon?" Aaron asked her as they spooned the delicious hot soup into their mouths.

"I'm reading a good book, but if you have something else planned, I'm up for it."

"While you read, I'm going to work on a project I'm doing for the local schools," said Aaron. "It's a history of the Abenaki tribe. It's the one Hazel talked me into doing for her class."

"That sounds terrific," Sarah said. She liked that they didn't have to do everything together.

###

Sarah was involved in her book when Aaron sat down beside her. "How's the book?"

"It's really interesting," she said, suddenly aware it was growing dark outside. "I didn't realize it was so late."

"It's time to get ready for cocktails and dinner. Mary Lou made us a lasagna unless you want something fancier."

"Lasagna sounds perfect. I'm going to freshen up," Sarah said, noticing Aaron's hair still a little wet from a shower. He'd changed into a black V-neck sweater and jeans which looked sexy on him.

He stood and pulled her up into his arms. "You look fine to me. But while you're gone, I'll open some wine for us. I also have some cheese and crackers."

"Sounds delicious. I'll be right back."

A few minutes later, when Sarah walked into the kitchen, Aaron let out a low whistle. "You look amazing."

She'd changed into a pair of black wool slacks and the green sweater she liked. To match the sparkles in the sweater, she'd brushed her hair back from her face and added dangly earrings.

"That's about as dressed up as I can get here in the woods," she teased.

Aaron handed her a glass of red wine. "Here's to a Happy New Year and the rest of the weekend."

"I can't think of a better way to spend it than to be here with you. It's been a special day. I really appreciate it."

"I'm glad you like being here," Aaron said, and Sarah knew how important it was to him.

###

Later, as the time headed closer to midnight, Sarah got up off the couch where they'd been watching a movie and went to get the two paper party hats and several rolling noisemakers she'd brought with her.

"I thought we could have some fun with these," Sarah said plopping a paper crown on his head.

Aaron picked up one of the noisemakers she handed him and blew on it, tickling her cheek with the feather at the end of it.

Laughing, Sarah did the same to him.

A harmless battle broke out, sending them into gales of laughter.

"Oops! We're almost missing the countdown," said Aaron.

On the television, an on-air party was counting down to one, then a barrage of fireworks went off.

Aaron drew Sarah to him and gave her a kiss that deepened as she wrapped her arms around his neck.

When they pulled apart, Aaron said, "I want this to be a special New Year for you and the girls. For us."

"Me, too," she said. "For all of us."

She waited for Aaron to say how much he loved her, but he'd already turned off the television and announced he was ready for bed.

He held out his hand to her and she took it, but doubts pushed in when he didn't declare his feelings.

CHAPTER TWENTY-FOUR

"SHOULD WE TAKE AN AFTERNOON WALK?" ASKED SARAH, coming out of the shower. "It's lovely out, with snow still falling."

"Sure, if you want to," said Aaron, wrapping a towel around her. "You can try using snowshoes again. Enough snow has fallen that it will be better to use them. That will allow us to go off the paths I've made with the snowplow. And I want to show you something."

Sarah understood that being outdoors was important to Aaron no matter the season. He was at peace when he was in nature, something she thought the girls would benefit from.

It took a while to get bundled up. She sat outside on the porch steps and attached her snowshoes, excited to be active in an entirely different way enjoying winter weather.

She stood. The sun sent light glistening against the snow, making her grateful she'd thought to bring sunglasses.

"You ready?" asked Aaron, looking delicious in his gray Irish sweater and blue jeans. He stood on his snowshoes and held out a gloved hand to her. "We'll leave the dogs behind so they can't ruin the clear snow for us."

She took his hand. It had been a fabulous two days and nights together and she was sorry she had to face reality and return to her work at the store tomorrow after just one more night with Aaron. This morning they'd talked and talked.

She'd quizzed Aaron about his thoughts on raising children, and they'd discussed every other topic they could think of until they were both satisfied with the idea of moving ahead with their relationship. Her doubts from the night before calmed.

They entered the woods quietly and moved in sync until Aaron wanted more exercise and went ahead. Sarah was content to follow. Out of the corner of her eye, she saw something move and turned to see a rabbit hopping in the snow. She let out a sigh of contentment at such an innocent sight. Though Aaron's cabin was a short drive from the town of Lilac Lake, it seemed to her they were on a planet of their own.

She heard a loud crack and looked up. The snow on top of the bare tree limbs was melting in the sun, making the branches heavier.

Concerned, she called out to Aaron and went in the direction he'd gone, moving faster and faster when she heard no response.

The stillness became eerie.

Her heart pumped with worry.

She came to an abrupt stop and let out a scream.

Aaron was lying face down in the snow next to a broken tree branch.

Sarah's body froze while her mind played nasty tricks with her, seeing Jesse all over again lying in the woods, his head bleeding from a gaping hole. Feeling sick to her stomach, Sarah bent over and gagged.

She was unaware of the tears streaming down her face as she raced to Aaron, crying out, "Aaron! Oh my God, Aaron!"

Gently, she rolled his body over, and saw where the

branch had hit his head. There was an ugly, bloody bump on it. She stared into his blank eyes and started screaming, "Oh, no! Please, Aaron. Wake up!"

She patted his cheek.

He stirred and then closed his eyes.

She checked to see if he'd been hit anywhere else, but she saw no signs of it.

Remembering finding Jesse and all those gory details, she lowered her face into her hands.

Shaking, feeling sick, she threw her arms around Aaron. "Wake up! Open your eyes!" She reached into her pocket for her cell phone and realized she'd left it on the kitchen counter.

Sobbing uncontrollably now, she tried Aaron's pocket and found his cell phone. She struggled to come up with a password to open it and tried as many dates as possible, until she hit on 0125. Her birthday.

Aaron began to groan.

Keeping an eye on him, Sarah called 911 and told them what had happened and where they were.

Kneeling in the snow beside him, she took hold of his hand and squeezed it, speaking softly in his ear. "You've been hit by a heavy branch. Help is on the way. I'm staying right with you. Aaron.... I... I love you."

He remained still, eyes closed.

Sarah had no idea how long they'd stayed like that until she finally heard the sound of someone calling her name.

Sarah stood. "Over here."

Two figures appeared. One was carrying something, a stretcher maybe. The other had hold of what looked like a suitcase, which she thought held medical supplies.

"Hurry! He has a bad gash on his head, and he won't wake

up. I don't think he has any other injuries, but I tried not to move him too much." She realized tears were sliding down her cheeks.

"Okay, we'll take it from here," said one of the EMTs.

Sarah stood aside clutching her gloved hands, telling herself it was Aaron on the ground, not Jesse, and that he'd be alright. Still, unwanted visions filled her mind. When was the last time she'd told Jesse she'd loved him? Was that the last thing she'd said to him? She'd had a habit of saying it to him a lot because he'd needed it so much.

"He's awake," she heard one of the EMTs say.

Sarah hurried over to them. "Please, let me see him."

She knelt beside Aaron and felt a rush of relief fill her when his eyes focused on her.

"Hi," he said. "What happened?"

"A heavy branch fell on your head," she said. "We've got people here to help you."

She kissed his cheek and stood, letting the men continue to care for Aaron. After checking his pulse and other vital signs, one of them worked on the head wound.

"He'll need stitches," the man declared.

In time, they allowed Aaron to sit up.

"You're a lucky man. Your wife called us," said one of the men.

Aaron groaned but sat holding his head in his hands. "No, just a friend."

At his words, Sarah felt a stab go through her heart. She told herself not to make anything of it, that Aaron had just had an injury to his head. But a sneaky thought grabbed onto the idea of her just being a friend, and all of her previous doubts roared back to life.

"Do you feel strong enough to stand?" one of the EMTs asked Aaron. "We need to get a professional to look at you."

"I'll walk," said Aaron looking at the folded stretcher one of the men had carried.

With help, Aaron struggled to his feet.

"I'll walk him to the ambulance," said one of the men. "Can someone carry my case?"

"I will," said Sarah, grateful to have something to do.

The four of them traveled slowly back to the cabin, where the ambulance was parked.

Following behind, Sarah kept her eye on the others. It was difficult to see Aaron, who was such an outdoorsman, moving like an old man. She still didn't know everything that might be wrong with him.

When they got to the ambulance, one of the men said to her, "We'll take him to Dr. Chambers Emergency Center, and he can decide whether the patient should be seen at a hospital."

"Okay, I'll meet you there. But first let me say goodbye to him."

Aaron was sitting by the open back door of the Ambulance. He seemed dazed as she approached him.

"I'll see you at Dr. Chambers's office." She looked into Aaron's eyes and kissed him on the cheek.

While one of the men helped Aaron into the ambulance, Sarah raced inside the cabin to get her phone and purse, then hurried to her car. She felt as if her feet were made of lead.

At the Emergency Center Emmett Chambers had set up at his office, Sarah stood in the waiting room, too upset to sit.

She knew Aaron was alive and able to move and talk, but she couldn't erase the scene of him lying in the snow from her mind. She needed to know if he'd have any side effects from the injury. And she couldn't help wondering if he'd heard her say that she loved him and what that might mean if he only considered her a friend. Was he reconsidering their talk about a future together?

Crystal was working at the front desk saying goodbye to someone who'd come into the Emergency Center with a broken finger. A nurse was assisting Emmett as he checked over Aaron.

The creation of an Emergency Center was Emmett's idea. He was often awakened in the night or disturbed at mealtime with one emergency after another, so he decided to expand his practice by hiring two additional nurses to help with coverage of all hours. By dividing coverage among them, it gave him more personal freedom and yet provided services when needed. Many of the so-called emergencies required the care of a nurse, not a doctor. Those that were more serious, Emmett took care of.

When Crystal was through with the mother and son she'd been working with, she came over to Sarah. "Are you okay? I heard Aaron's arrival."

Sarah started to speak, then stopped to catch her breath. Her heart was pounding so hard she could hardly speak. "It was so horrible. Aaron lying on the snow. It was almost like seeing Jesse all over again."

Crystal studied her with sympathy and wrapped her arms around Sarah. "Why don't you sit? What can I bring you to drink? Water? Coffee? Tea?"

"Water would be perfect, thank you. I just have to make

sure Aaron is going to be okay. You know?"

"Yes," said Crystal. "I understand. You and Aaron are close."

Sarah held back fresh tears. They were so much more than just close. He was the soulmate she never should've left.

Emmett came to the doorway. "Sarah? Aaron wants to speak to you."

"How is he?" Sarah asked.

"He's going to be fine, but he's had a serious blow to his head. I've stitched up the wound, but he says you'll take care of him from here. I need to be sure that you can manage."

Sarah followed Emmett into an examination room.

Aaron sat on an exam table and studied her with an apologetic look. "I hope you don't mind keeping an eye on me like the doctor requested."

"Of course not," said Sarah, going to him and giving him a hug. She pulled away. "Does it hurt? Can you remember anything about the injury?"

Aaron shook his head. "No. Not until the EMTs were checking me over and then everything has been sort of foggy since then. Sorry I ruined the afternoon."

"The important thing is that you're okay. You scared me so." Sarah glanced at Emmett.

As if he could read her mind, he gave her a look of understanding and quietly said, "This situation is very different from the one you had with your husband."

"What is it that you need me to do?" Sarah asked Emmett.

"For the next several days, I need you to keep an eye on him. He's had a concussion, and I want to be sure we didn't miss anything. Effects are often short term and can include headaches and trouble with concentration, memory, balance, mood, and sleep. Aaron will need plenty of rest, and I don't want him to be alone. I will prescribe medicine for the headaches, but we don't like to over prescribe."

"Okay," said Sarah. "I can do this. Aaron can stay at my house when I leave the cabin tomorrow. And when I'm at the store, my daytime sitter can be available to be with him."

"Oh, right. That will work. Aaron said you'd been staying with him for the holiday weekend," said Emmett. He gave Aaron a steady look. "I'm your doctor and I expect you to follow my instructions. I know that you're normally an active man, but rest is extremely important for a healthy recovery. Understood?"

"Yes, I get it. I'll do as you say if it means I can get better sooner." Aaron returned Emmett's steady gaze.

"We used to think it was important for someone not to sleep so much following an injury like this, but that has changed. We want our patients to give the body time to heal," said Emmett.

"We'll go back to the cabin, and then tomorrow Aaron can temporarily move in with me," said Sarah. Earlier, Aaron and Sarah had talked about when Aaron would be able to spend the night at her house, and though this wasn't the way she wanted, having him there might be a test for the girls.

Emmett shook hands with Aaron. "Let me know if either of you has any concerns. For now, give your body a rest and let it heal."

When they returned to the waiting area, Crystal was there with paperwork for Aaron to sign. Since the sale of the Lilac Lake Café, she'd worked hard to help Emmett set up the clinic and remained a true partner in her husband's business.

As they left the office, Sarah took hold of Aaron's hand

and was both surprised and pleased that he allowed her to lead him to her car. Sarah knew then how much Aaron had suffered from the injury.

CHAPTER TWENTY-FIVE

BACK AT THE CABIN, THE SUN WAS MAKING ITS WAY TO THE horizon ending the brightness of earlier. Sarah let the dogs outside. Though they raced out the door, they soon came back in to be with Aaron, aware something was wrong.

Aaron lay on the couch gently rubbing their ears, and they found places to sit nearby. Even Luke joined the watchful group of canines.

Sarah cleaned up the breakfast and lunch dishes and then checked to see what she'd brought for dinner. She'd ordered a lot of meals from the Lilac Lake Café and was now pleased she'd splurged. She wanted this last night at the cabin to be special.

While Aaron slept, Sarah read one of her favorite author's new books, frequently checking to see that Aaron was alright.

Later, Sarah served supper on the coffee table in the living room so they could eat in front of the fire.

"I was going to serve champagne tonight," said Aaron. "We'll have that another time."

"Hot tea tastes nice on an evening like this," said Sarah. "The important thing is for you to get better. You gave me a fright."

"I'm sure I did," said Aaron. "It happened so fast I couldn't move out of the way. I'm sorry to ruin our time together like this."

"How do you feel about having to move in with me for a few days? Does that add any pressure on you? I don't want you to make more of it than just a friend helping a friend," said Sarah. She held her breath, waiting for his reaction.

"Yes, that will keep us both comfortable around the girls," said Aaron.

Sarah sighed, more confused than ever about their relationship.

The next morning, Sarah called her mother, who was watching the girls, and told her about Aaron's accident and that he was staying with her on Dr. Chambers' orders.

Her mother said, "Isn't that a little premature? Having him spend nights with you with the girls there?"

Sarah held back her temper. She'd gone through hell in the last two days, and she wasn't going to worry what her neighbors may or may not think about it.

"Mom, this isn't the fifties, where things like that were important. Nothing inappropriate will take place in front of the girls. They like Aaron, and this will give Aaron and me an unexpected opportunity to see how things go with us all together."

"I understand," said her mother. "Is Aaron going to be alright? Was it horrible?"

"Seeing him lying face down in the snow was terrible," admitted Sarah. "That's why I feel it's important for me to see that he heals well. As Dr. Chambers said, this is an entirely different story with a different outcome for me than I had with Jesse. I need to do this."

"I'm here to help as much as I can, but I'll be busy getting ready for the winter move to Florida."

"Yes, I know," said Sarah. "Lucy and Millie are willing to help during the day. And don't forget we have our meeting with the lawyer to go over the arrangement with Dani. She and I have been busy all week preparing a year-end inventory check, which will help with the evaluation of the business. Wyatt and April have been helping and will do extra work for us. They're anxious to earn the money."

"You have a lot on your plate, right now. But I'm sure you can handle it." Sarah wished she was as confident about that as her mother.

Sarah was relieved her mother wouldn't return the girls until after she'd settled Aaron into the house. She was concerned about having his two dogs join Luke, but when they were led inside, all three were eager to go out to the backyard while she brought in suitcases and unpacked the groceries she'd picked up before coming home.

Her cabin had a master suite and two bedrooms, one smaller than the other that Sarah sometimes used as an office. She'd put a daybed in the office for guests, and it was in this room that Aaron took his suitcase.

"It's comfortable," said Sarah. "You're free to use either the girls' bathroom or mine. The little half-bath is also nearby."

She went to the closet and pulled out a couple of pillows, a duvet, and a quilt. "You have your choice." She gazed around the room and frowned. "It's not as much space as you're used to."

"This is going to be just fine," said Aaron. "I'm glad for the privacy."

"The girls can be overwhelming at times. Feel free to let them know when you need to be by yourself. The purpose of having you here is to rest."

Aaron pulled her to him. "You are my purpose in being here. I want to get well for you, so we can continue our relationship. So-called friends or not."

Sarah couldn't help the smile she felt curving her lips. "Your priority has to be your healing. I'll wait for the other."

His lips lowered onto hers and she felt herself going back to the evenings at the cabin when kisses were just the beginning.

"Hello? Is anyone here?" called her mother, sending Aaron and Sarah spinning apart as if they were the high school sweethearts they'd been.

"Mommy! Where's Aaron?" called Mia.

"Hi, Mommy," said Emily rushing into her arms while Mia hugged Aaron around his legs.

"Is Aaron going to sleep in here?" asked Emily. She went over to him. "Did you bump your head?"

He pointed to the bandage on his head. "A branch fell on it."

"Is that why you're sleeping here?" asked Mia, studying his head.

"You can sleep with my Teddy bear," said Emily.

"And my doggy," said Mia.

They both ran out of the room.

Sarah's mother came to the doorway. "I'm sorry to hear about your injury, Aaron. If there's anything I can do for you, please let me know."

"Thank you," said Aaron. "This is a perfect set-up for me here. And Mary Lou will no doubt come for visits. I understand you and Bob are getting ready to leave for Florida."

"Yes. With the doctor's approval, we'll leave mid-January."

"I promise to keep an eye on Sarah and give her a hand whenever she needs me to," said Aaron.

Seeing him bandaged and obviously not himself, it sounded a bit silly. But Sarah knew he'd keep his word. She walked with her mother into the kitchen.

"Care for a cup of coffee or tea? You must be tired."

Her mother laughed. "I admit I am, but we had a lot of fun with the girls for New Year's Eve complete with hats, noisemakers, and treats. We celebrated at ten o'clock because we were too tired to stay awake."

"You're such a good grandmother," said Sarah, giving her mother a quick hug of gratitude.

Sarah fixed coffee for her mother and herself, and when she went to ask Aaron what he might like, she found him sleeping on top of the daybed, a Teddy bear and stuffed dog beside him.

Deeply touched by her daughters' kindnesses, Sarah tiptoed out of the room and closed the door.

Later, in the girls' room, Sarah talked to them about their weekend and learned that they, as usual, had had a fun time.

"Starting tomorrow we have to get in our school routine," said Sarah. "And then in a couple of weeks, we'll have another routine when your grandparents go to Florida."

"We know, Mom," said Mia. "Mimi already invited us to visit in Florida."

"To see the beach," Emily added.

Sarah was surprised. It was hard keeping up with these two.

"Now that Aaron is staying with us for a few days, I want you to remember he has to get lots of rest. So, no fighting and fussing around him."

"Is he going to be our daddy?" asked Mia, settling a gaze on Sarah.

"He's a friend, a good friend," said Sarah hoping to put an end to the conversation. "Guess what's for dinner. Lasagna that Mrs. Collister made. It's delicious."

"Yay," cried the girls together, their voices blending beautifully.

Satisfied that she'd reconnected with the girls, Sarah left their room and went to the kitchen to organize supper. She saw the opened bottle of wine she'd brought from the cabin and poured herself a glass, unwilling to end what was supposed to be a romantic weekend. If she was honest with herself, she'd even hoped Aaron might profess his love. But that seemed a long time from happening.

She set the table for dinner and stood back gazing at it. Settings for four seemed so right. But she'd have to be careful how she handled Aaron's presence. She didn't want to mislead the girls in any way.

Aaron walked into the kitchen and sat down at the table. "Wow! I have a headache. Where is the medicine Dr. Chambers gave me?"

"It's right here in the cupboard. Stay there. I'll bring it and a glass of water to you."

"Thanks." He gave her a weak smile. "I appreciate being here. I hope it won't be too much trouble for you. I know you have your own life and are busy with the kids."

Sarah got Aaron the medicine and water and brought it to him. She looked into his eyes. "I'm glad to do this for you, Aaron."

"Okay. Things suddenly seem a little off with me crowding into your home..."

Sarah's fingers turned ice cold. "Are you having second thought about our relationship?"

His eyes widened. "No, why would you say that?"

Sarah drew a deep breath and decided not to hold back her hurt. "When the EMTs thought I was your wife, you told them very plainly that I was just a friend. I'm not your wife, but I hope I'm more than 'just a friend'."

"Come here," said Aaron, drawing her into his lap. "I didn't really know what I was saying. You're much more than that."

She nestled against him, loving the solid feel of him. It would take some time before she got over the unbelievable sight of him sprawled on the ground like her dead husband, leaving her with too many uncertain feelings.

After an uneventful night in which Sarah, the girls, Aaron, and the dogs had an uninterrupted sleep, Sarah got up ready to get back to her usual routine. She couldn't allow the fact that Aaron was in the house to stop her from taking care of her business. Not when her parents were about to leave her handling the store.

Luke left the girls' room and followed Sarah to the kitchen

where she let him out to the backyard. Soon Knight and Coal came into the kitchen, and she let them out.

While she was standing at the sliding door watching them play, she felt rather than heard Aaron approach. She turned around. "'Morning. Did you sleep well?"

"Not really," Aaron said. "I figure I can take a nap today." He kissed her. "It was hard knowing you were asleep a couple of rooms away."

She gave him a teasing grin. "I can't believe I slept well."

He chuckled. "I'm going to grab a drink of water and go back to bed. It might be easier if I'm out of the way. I don't want to disrupt their routine."

"Can I bring you anything else? Something to eat?"

"No, this will be fine. I can find something to eat a little later. I'm feeling a little nauseous."

Aaron headed back to his room, and Sarah went to wake the girls.

Later, as the girls sat at the table eating their breakfast, Mia said, "Do we have to go to school? Why can't we stay here with Aaron?"

"Aaron needs quiet time to rest and get better. A little later, Lucy is going to come and stay at the house until it's time to pick you up."

"Can we say goodbye to him?" asked Emily.

"If he's awake, you can go in his room and tell him," Sarah said. She was beginning to wonder if this idea of Aaron staying with them was a good idea. The girls were getting too attached to him.

After the girls were dressed and Sarah was ready to leave with them, she allowed the girls to check on Aaron. Both of his dogs were lying on the floor by his bed. When they saw the girls, they got up and went over to greet them, wagging their tails.

Aaron sat up. "Ready for school?" he asked the girls.

"Yes, but we want to say goodbye," said Mia.

Unprepared for two girls racing to him and giving him hugs, he was thrown back against the pillow. The girls left him as quickly as they'd arrived.

Sarah watched him closely to see his reaction.

Aaron drew a deep breath, clutched his head, and managed to smile.

Relieved, Sarah gave him a little wave. "We'll see you later today. Lucy should arrive by ten o'clock. She's promised to help but will stay out of your way."

"Thanks for everything," Aaron said, leaning back against the pillow.

Sarah piled the girls into the car and drove them to their preschool. There, she parked and got out of the car thinking it might be smart to tell the teachers why Aaron was staying with them.

Inside, one of the teachers came over to her. "I heard from a neighbor that Aaron was brought to the emergency clinic with a concussion. Is he alright?"

"Hard to keep anything quiet in this town, huh?" said Sarah.

The teacher gave her a knowing look. "That's Lilac Lake."

Chuckling, Sarah said, "I thought I should let you know that Aaron is staying with the girls and me for a few days to get some rest. That's all it is."

"Okay, thanks for telling us," said the teacher. "I assume

Lucy will pick up the girls this afternoon."

"Right. Thanks," said Sarah, glad to get the correct details of Aaron's stay out to the public.

Dani was already inside turning on the store lights when Sarah arrived. Sarah grinned. She'd been right about making Dani part of the ownership. She was a loyal, hard worker.

"Glad to see you here," said Sarah. "Sorry I'm late. I was held up at the girls' preschool."

Dani gave her a look of concern. "How's Aaron? I heard about his accident and that he's staying with you."

Sarah let out a long sigh. "I guess everyone knows he's at my house. He's going to be fine, but he took a significant bump on the head and needs lots of rest. And Emmett said he didn't want Aaron to be alone. My babysitter for the girls is coming to stay at my house until I get home from work."

"How are you doing?" Dani asked. "It must have been frightening."

"I was really shaken by seeing him lying in the snow. It reminded me so much of how I found my husband. But I'm glad I was there, so I could get help for him. He was unconscious for several minutes. That's why it's so important for him not to be left alone."

Dani's lips curved into a wicked smile. "So, what's it like to have a man around the house again?"

Sarah laughed. "It's a test for him to see how to deal with children. I just don't want the girls to be disappointed when the time comes for him to leave."

"Maybe it's wise of you to have him stay a while," said Dani. "It'll give him an idea of how it might be going forward.

By the way, how did you like the cabin? You haven't seen it since all the upgrades and additions."

Sarah clapped a hand to her chest. "It's amazing. I had no idea it was so luxurious."

"Once I talked Aaron into making the additions, he became excited by the concept. He's content to have little, but the idea of the cabin becoming a family home really caught his attention."

"He said you sometimes show it to potential customers," Sarah said.

"Yes. It gave us a chance to try out some new ideas." Dani gave her a quick hug. "It would be fantastic if you and the girls ended up living there someday."

"Whoa!" said Sarah. "Aaron told the EMTs we were just friends. He doesn't remember doing it, but it's made me realize not to take anything for granted." At the look of disbelief on Dani's face, Sarah held up her hands. "I know, I know. I shouldn't rush to judgement, but I don't want the girls or me to get hurt."

"I don't believe that's going to happen but better to be safe than sorry. It hasn't been very long since you guys officially made the decision to be together," said Dani. "One more bit of news. You know how Tessa always talked about finding a man."

"Yes. It was always so annoying," said Sarah. "She was very interested in Aaron."

"It seems that she was caught stealing from guests over the New Year's s weekend. I don't have all the details. Just that she was fired, and Melissa is helping out at the Inn until they hire someone to take Tessa's place permanently."

"Enough people were put off by Tessa that we should've

known she had some real problems," said Sarah. "We're usually an inviting group."

"Yeah, we are," said Dani. "Blake has stepped right into our circle. Everyone likes him. Poppy most of all."

Sarah felt a smile cross her face. "I have a feeling that a Lilac Lake wedding will take place this year and Poppy will end up moving back into her old house."

"I hope so," said Dani. "They make a great couple."

"And I adore April. She's a wonderful girl."

"Agreed," said Dani.

A customer came to the front door, and their conversation ended.

There was no further talk about Aaron as the day took shape. Both she and Dani remained busy looking over figures. They drew up a list of items to order as they discovered empty places in their merchandise.

In the afternoon, Wyatt and April came into work and were sent to two different areas to start counting merchandise to compare with the computerized sheets.

By the time Sarah headed home, she was tired and a little grumpy. She hated doing an inventory of the store because they carried several thousand items from small screws to lawnmowers and grills.

CHAPTER TWENTY-SIX

SARAH PULLED INTO THE DRIVEWAY AND WAS PLEASED to see the lights on in the living room welcoming her. And when she opened the front door and three dogs greeted her, she couldn't help but grin.

Lucy came out of the kitchen. "Oh, good. You're home. I'm sorry but I have to leave right away. There's an important meeting at The Woodlands, and I promised to attend. It's been a pleasant day. Aaron is delightful, and the girls adore him."

Lucy left, and Sarah made her way into the kitchen to find the table set and dinner ready to cook on top of the oven.

As she texted a thank you to Lucy, Aaron came into the room. "Lucy made one of her favorite casseroles for dinner. The girls are playing in their rooms. And I fed the dogs."

"Wow. That's so helpful," Sarah said, kissing him. "I've forgotten what it's like to have this kind of partnership. How are you doing?"

Aaron shrugged. "I'm frustrated by being so inactive, but I know Emmett is right about my needing rest. Whenever I try to do too much, I end up with a bad headache."

The girls walked into the room dressed up in costumes. Her mother had given the girls a cardboard chest filled with old clothes and jewelry she'd bought for them to play with.

"Hi, Mommy!" said Emily, wearing a dress and a string of fake pearls. "I'm a teacher. Like Ms. Cherie."

"And I'm a cowgirl," said Mia. She wore a cowboy hat, a fringed skirt, and cowboy boots Sarah's mother had picked out.

Sarah laughed and gave them each a hug. "We'll be eating dinner in a little while. So, you're free to play some more."

"Come play with us, Aaron," Mia said.

He shook his head. "I already did. It's time for me to talk with your mother."

"Okay," said Emily. "Maybe you will read us a book at bedtime."

Aaron ruffled her hair. "Okay."

Sarah slid the casserole into the oven and turned to Aaron. "I'm going to have a glass of wine. Would you like one?"

"Yes. Emmett called to see how I'm doing. I asked him about having alcohol. He said a small amount was okay. He also suggested I stay here with you for at least a couple more days. He's pushing that idea because I didn't make a trip to a hospital, and he wants to be overly cautious."

She poured wine into two glasses, handed him one, then sat at the kitchen table opposite him.

"How did your day go?" she asked.

"Lucy's really nice and was there whenever I needed anything. She said she likes fussing over people. You're lucky to have her babysit for the girls."

"I think so too. How were the girls today?" Sarah asked. "A little too rambunctious for you?"

"They're active girls," Aaron said. "You've done a nice job with them."

Sarah smiled at him. "Thanks. That means a lot."

"Did you find everything you needed here at the house?"

Sarah asked. At his nod, she continued. "By the way, I told the girls' teachers you were staying here to recuperate. That's all."

He studied her with a puzzled expression. "I guess we don't want anyone to get the wrong idea about us. Right?" His tone had an edge to it.

"We may have tried to rush things earlier. I don't want you to feel pressured into anything. And I certainly don't want the girls to get hurt."

Aaron looked away and studied the outdoors through the sliding glass door which led to the deck and beyond it to the woods and the river. When he turned back to her, his eyes held a sadness she hadn't seen in a long time. "I thought we had something special, Sarah."

"I did too, but then you mentioned we were just friends, and I realized that was true. We're friends. Good friends. Valued friends."

"I thought you wanted more than that," Aaron said.

"I do, but I'll wait until I know for sure that you do too before I announce it to anyone else."

Aaron studied her but didn't say anything.

Sarah had too much on her mind to worry about it. Dani's partnership needed to be settled, and she had to help her parents take off to Florida as they wanted. All that was between them staying here and their departure was her father's visit to the doctor. She'd admit it to no one, but she was nervous about it. What if her father wasn't okay? Or what if the doctor gave the go-ahead and something awful happened to him in Florida?

Dinner was a reasonably quiet affair. The girls were tired from going back to preschool after a long break and conversation was merely polite between Aaron and her.

After dinner, Sarah got the girls in the bathtub and later, in their nightgowns they raced to Aaron's room.

"Story time!" announced Mia.

"Will you read us this book? Please?" Emily said.

"Sure," said Aaron.

Mia and Emily sat on either side of him and leaned in to look at the book about a bear roaming around a shopping mall at night. The sight touched Sarah's heart.

When he was through reading the book, Mia said, "One more."

Sarah waited to see what he would say.

"Not tonight. Maybe another time. I'm tired," said Aaron.

"Remember Aaron needs his rest," said Sarah, leading the girls to the bathroom before taking them to bed.

In their bedroom, the girls lay back on their pillows.

" 'Night, sweet girls. I'll see you in the morning. I love you."

"I love you more," the girls recited together.

"I love you to the moon and back," Sarah said, nuzzling each girls' neck and kissing her cheek.

Sarah left the door open a crack as they liked, ready for adult time.

She knocked on Aaron's door. "Want to relax before the fire for a while?"

He got up. "Sure. Maybe we can talk."

They walked into the living room and moved a few dogs out of the way to sit on the couch in front of the fire.

Aaron put his arm around Sarah and let out a long sigh. "I've been thinking about what you said about being friends, valuable friends. I know what I want, and it's more than that. But I'm going to give you time to think about it. Right now, you're scared to get hurt because of something I said. You need to trust me more than that. I know you've been hurt in the past, but as Emmett said, this is a different situation with a different outcome. You have to believe it."

Sarah knew Aaron was right. She had to feel more secure in their relationship. She didn't realize what damage his one comment had done to her self-confidence or the feeling of being loved by Aaron. Jesse had done more to destroy her than she'd thought. Maybe it was time to go back to another counseling session.

Still, she allowed him to draw her into his arms. And when he kissed her, she felt the heat of it down to the tips of her toes. The chemistry between them was there. No problem.

"It'll be all right," Aaron whispered into her ear.

At his sweet gentleness, she let out a sigh. She wanted him. She wanted him to be part of her family. She wanted to be free of the past.

The next day, she kissed Aaron and left with the girls for another busy day at the store. She warned him that she would be home late, that she was attending a counseling session.

"No problem. Lucy and I or one of us will be here for the girls," said Aaron.

"Thanks." It still surprised and pleased her that he was so willing to help.

The girls said goodbye to her at their school and Sarah hurried along to the store. She and Dani had talked about implementing winter hours, and as she drove there, Sarah thought it was a smart idea. They could open at nine and close at five. Contractors could call for an emergency opening.

Sarah arrived at the empty store and opened it up, turning on lights, getting the cash register set, and making sure everything was ready to go.

While she waited for the day to begin, she fixed herself a cup of coffee.

Dani arrived. Instead of her usual cheerful greeting, she said nothing.

Seeing the way Dani's eyes were red and swollen, Sarah said, "What's wrong? Can I help?"

"I'm not pregnant. I'll be better, but right now I just need not to talk about it," said Dani.

Sarah gave her a hug and walked away. She understood how disappointed Dani was. Her thoughts flew to Mia and Emily. They were so precious to her. After their birth, she and Jesse hadn't tried for other children, had, in fact, refrained from making love more often than not because he was not doing well. Nothing she did seemed to help.

The day was a slow one, for which Sarah was grateful. It gave her time to prepare figures and ideas for the meeting between Dani, her parents, and herself.

Because it was so slow, Dani left the store early, leaving the regular staffer to handle things. April was also trained to handle the cash register and was eager to take over whenever needed.

After she closed the store, Sarah went to see Dr. Ellen Fitzpatrick, who ran the grief sessions and was also Sarah's counselor. She was a lovely woman in her early fifties, with frosted brown hair, bright blue eyes that seemed to reach inside people and draw them out, and a kindness that wreathed her face with a glow.

More than that, Dr. Fitzpatrick was a realist. She understood what people were going through and was clear about healthy ways to deal with it. Sarah had trusted her enough to decide to make the move to Lilac Lake, after her parents wanted her back in town. This last bump in letting go of her past was the most important to Sarah, because she truly wanted to move forward with Aaron.

When she arrived at Dr. Fitzpatrick's office, a client was leaving through another door.

Dr. Fitzpatrick appeared in the waiting room. "Good timing. Come on in, Sarah, and let's talk."

Once they were both seated in comfortable chairs facing one another, Dr. Fitzpatrick gave Sarah a steady look. "What brings you here today? You seemed stressed on the phone when you called for an appointment."

"You know that Aaron and I have been seeing one another. I spent New Year's Eve weekend with him."

Dr. Fitzpatrick gave her an encouraging look.

"Aaron was involved in an accident. A heavy tree limb snapped in the winter storm and hit him on the head. When one of the EMTs referred to me as his wife, Aaron quickly informed them that I was just a friend."

"And how did that make you feel?" Dr. Fitzpatrick asked.

"Betrayed," said Sarah so swiftly that she surprised herself. "We'd just spent the weekend together which was very nice, very romantic. And it made me remember how Jesse would accept or reject me at times. Aaron says I have to learn to trust him, but he hasn't even mentioned anything permanent."

"Has he shown you that he's serious?" asked Dr. Fitzpatrick.

"Yes. Many times."

"Has he given you a reason not to trust him, other than his statement about being just friends?" asked Dr. Fitzpatrick.

"No," Sarah admitted. "So many times I've envisioned our being a family—Aaron, the girls, and me. They love him."

"And do you?" asked Dr. Fitzpatrick.

Sarah slumped in her chair. "Yes, I do. I just question whether it will last. But Aaron and I have been given a second chance, and I don't want to lose that."

"You have your answer, Sarah. As always, follow your instincts and your heart. You have good ones."

Sarah gave her a thoughtful nod. "Thank you so much for listening to me. It always helps."

"Good luck, Sarah. You're a wonderful woman and an excellent mother."

Dr. Fitzpatrick stood, and Sarah realized her time was up.

She left and drove home feeling much better about her relationship with Aaron.

CHAPTER TWENTY-SEVEN

THE NEXT DAY, SARAH TOLD AARON THE STORE WOULD BE closing early, that she and Dani were meeting with her parents and a lawyer to draw up details for allowing Dani to buy into ownership of the store.

"I'll come home as soon as I can," Sarah assured him. "Is there anything I can do for you in the meantime? You seem to be getting better."

"I'm starting to feel more like myself. I think Dr. Chambers will agree that I can go home tomorrow."

"That will be a sad day for the girls and me," said Sarah. "It's been nice having you and the dogs here. We've all enjoyed it." She wrapped her arms around him, trying not to think how empty the house would be without him.

The girls hugged Aaron goodbye and then Sarah got them into the car to drive to their school.

"Why did Aaron say he was going home?" asked Mia.

"Why can't he stay with us forever and forever?" Emily asked.

"Aaron lives at his own house. He was just staying with us until his head injury got better," said Sarah.

"But I want him to be with us," said Mia.

"I know you do, but he has his own house to take care of. He can still come and visit us sometimes," Sarah said, feeling as unhappy about the situation as the girls. Even if she asked him to stay, she knew he wouldn't. He thought she needed time to trust him, but that wasn't the issue at all. It was her old wounds that had made both of them think that. But now she had a better understanding of the past and how it had affected her thinking about the future.

As she and Dani entered the lawyer's office with her parents, Sarah realized how much her life was about to change.

Seated on the opposite side of the conference table from her parents, she saw how much they'd each aged since her father had a stroke. It was as if time, that had been so gentle to them, had raced to make sure they now looked their age. She loved them. They deserved time away from the stress of the business, and owning part of the store meant that she had financial independence.

During the meeting, many topics were covered, including the subject of reducing store hours with no financial loss.

"With the Beckman Lumber Company opening early for the contractors and Home Depot in Concord, we don't need to try to compete with them. We're now offering more household items and services, and our customers don't usually shop until nine or ten in the morning," said Sarah.

"What are you saying?" her father asked her a bit defensively.

"I'm saying our customer base has changed within the last few years and our stock has changed to meet new customer demands. With Dani and me busy with our families, I think we should be open 9 to 5 during the week and Saturday, and 12 to 5 on Sunday."

Sarah's father stirred in his seat restlessly.

Her mother placed a hand on his arm to quiet him. "I think Sarah and Dani are right. When we opened all those years ago, it was a very different story."

"We can hire staff to come in for extra hours during town celebrations and the like," said Dani. "This store has been at the center of this town since before it became the sophisticated place it is today. The reputation you have built with it is the one reason I wanted to become part of it. To carry on what you've created."

Sarah gazed at her wide-eyed. No wonder Dani was such a whiz at consulting. Both her parents looked as if they were about to cry.

"Well, then," said her father. "It seems as if you two have thought of how you want to handle the store going forward."

"But if the numbers are affected by the shorter business day, we'll have to address that," said her mother.

"Of course. It'll be the four of us owning the business," said Sarah. "I'm so very grateful to you, Mom and Dad, and to you, Dani, for making this happen."

"Any other issues to resolve?" the lawyer asked, looking around the table. When nobody answered, he said, "Okay, let's continue with the signing. The rest is clearly stated."

After all the paperwork was signed, the four of them exchanged hugs and then Sarah said, "As long as the store is closed, I'm going home."

When she pulled into her driveway, she didn't see Lucy's car. Puzzled, she went inside.

"Hello?"

Aaron came out of the kitchen. “I’m here. Watching the kids play in the backyard. Lucy called to tell me she was sick, and I assured her I’d pick up the girls and watch them here. We didn’t want to bother you when I knew how important your meeting was today.”

“That’s so sweet of you. Thank you.” Sarah gave him a hug which turned into a kiss, which turned into a deepened kiss that made her knees go weak.

“I really missed our alone time,” she said, catching her breath.

They walked into the kitchen and gazed outside.

Simultaneously, they froze. The backyard was empty. No girls. No dogs.

“Oh, my God!” said Sarah. “Where are the girls?”

She dashed outside.

Studying the melting snow left behind after a couple of days of sunshine, Sarah saw footprints heading to the back gate. “They’ve escaped!” she cried, running to the gate which she could now see was unlatched.

Aaron was at her heels. “The river! The dogs love the water.”

In her haste, Sarah slid down the embankment, landing on her hands and knees. In the distance, she could see the bright pink jackets of the girls as they followed the dogs cavorting alongside the moving water.

“Girls! Stop!” she called, hurrying after them, slipping on some of the stones and rocks near the water’s edge.

She saw one pink jacket enter the water and cried, “No-o-o-o!”

Aaron swept by her and raced to where the girls and dogs had stopped. Seconds later, he was in the river, swimming after Mia who thrashed about in the water.

Luke followed him into the water while the other two dogs waded in.

Sarah reached them and saw that Emily was crying hysterically as she watched Aaron and Mia.

A few feet down the river's edge, Aaron emerged carrying Mia.

Sarah raced over to them, sobbing, "Oh, my God! Is she alright?"

"Quick, give me your coat for her. We need to get her up to the house to warm up."

"Mommy!" Mia cried, holding out her arms to her.

Sarah hugged her, wrapping her coat around her, but didn't take her in her arms. She knew Aaron was faster than she'd ever be.

Aaron took off at a run, his agility in full view as he danced around rocks and stones to get back to the house.

Sarah grabbed hold of Emily and followed as quickly as she could.

The dogs, including Luke, who was dripping wet, galloped ahead of her.

Aaron had left the sliding glass door open for them.

Once they were inside, Sarah closed and locked it. She could hear the sound of running water and found Aaron in the bathroom.

"We need to get her out of her wet clothes and let her soak in tepid water and then gradually raise the temperature."

Mia was sobbing and when she reached for her, Sarah, on her knees, hugged her tightly while Emily clung to her backside. "You're going to be alright, thanks to Aaron. Quickly, we need to get you warmed up. That river is dangerously cold."

"I want to get in, too," said Emily, taking off her clothes.

"Keep close to your sister," Sarah said, watching as the two of them clung to each other.

Aaron handed her his cell phone. "I've got Dr. Chambers office on the line."

"Thank you." Sarah took the phone and talked to the nurse, who conferred with Emmett.

When the nurse returned to the phone, she said, "Emmett says you're doing the right thing. Make her a hot cup of cocoa, keep her bundled up after she's out of the tub, and watch for any adverse effects. The fact that she was in the water for so little time is important."

Sarah sat next to the tub watching the girls, her heart still pounding at all she might've lost.

After they were out of the tub and dressed in warm pajamas, Sarah went to find Aaron.

"How are the girls?" he asked, looking worried. "I've gone outside and locked the gate. I also put an extra coil of wire around the gate latch and the post so it can't be opened again."

Sarah felt the floor give way beneath her feet. She hadn't realized she was falling until she felt Aaron's arms wrapped around her.

"Hey, steady there. It's okay now," Aaron said in a soothing tone.

Suddenly, all the emotions she'd stored inside to keep from frightening the girls emerged in loud, racking sobs that shook her body so hard Aaron had to hold on tight.

"You saved her! What would've happened if you weren't here? I don't know how you did it. We're so lucky you were here. It's where we want you all the time."

"It's where I want to be," said Aaron, giving her a loving gaze. "I love you, Sarah, and I love the girls."

She caressed his face between her hands. "You think I didn't trust you; but it was me. I didn't trust myself to show you how much I love you because I can't believe we're together again. It's what I've wanted for so long."

"It's what I've waited for," said Aaron.

"Is this what you call Love's Harvest? Letting our love grow like this?" she asked, staring into his dark eyes.

"You could say that. It's taken us years to get here, but it feels so right."

As his lips captured hers, they were unaware of the girls standing beside them until Emily said, "Kisses are good."

Sarah and Aaron pulled apart, and as if they'd orchestrated it before, each one pulled a girl up into an embrace until they were all hugging one another.

"Hugs are good too," said Sarah, wondering how she could be so lucky. She wasn't sure what the future would bring, but she knew the four of them could handle anything together because she and Aaron had harvested a lasting love.

# # # # #

Thank you for reading *Love's Harvest.* If you enjoyed this book, please help other readers discover it by leaving a review on Amazon, Goodreads, BookBub, or your favorite site. It's such a nice thing to do.

Sign up for my newsletter and get a free story. I keep my newsletters short and fun with giveaways, recipes, and the latest must-have news about me and my books. Welcome! Here's the link:

https://BookHip.com/RRGJKGN

About the Author

A *USA Today* Best-Selling Author, Judith Keim is a hybrid author who both has a publisher and self-publishes. Ms. Keim writes heart-warming novels about women who face unexpected challenges, meet them with strength, and find love and happiness along the way. Her best-selling books are based, in part, on many of the places she's lived or visited and on the interesting people she's met, creating believable characters and realistic settings her many loyal readers love. Ms. Keim loves to hear from her readers and appreciates their enthusiasm for her stories.

Ms. Keim enjoyed her childhood and young-adult years in Elmira, New York, and now makes her home in Boise, Idaho, with her husband and their lovable miniature Dachshund, Wally, and other members of her family.

While growing up, she was drawn to the idea of writing stories from a young age. Books were always present, being read, ready to go back to the library, or about to be discovered. All in her family shared information from the books in general conversation, giving them a wealth of knowledge and vivid imaginations.

"I hope you've enjoyed this book. If you have, please help other readers discover it by leaving a review on Amazon, Goodreads, Bookbub, or the site of your choice. And please check out my other books and series:"

The Hartwell Women Series

The Beach House Hotel Series

Fat Fridays Group

The Salty Key Inn Series

The Chandler Hill Inn Series

Seashell Cottage Books

The Desert Sage Inn Series

Soul Sisters at Cedar Mountain Lodge

The Sanderling Cove Inn Series

The Lilac Lake Inn Series

The Lilac Lake Books

"ALL THE BOOKS ARE NOW AVAILABLE IN AUDIO on Audible, iTunes, Findaway, Kobo and Google Play! So fun to have these characters come alive!"

Ms. Keim can be reached at **www.judithkeim.com**

And to like her author page on Facebook and keep up with the news, go to: **http://bit.ly/2pZWDgA**

To receive notices about new books, follow her on Book Bub: **https://www.bookbub.com/authors/judith-keim**

And here's a link to where you can sign up for her periodic newsletter! **http://bit.ly/2OQsb7s**

She is also on Twitter @judithkeim, LinkedIn, and Goodreads. Come say hello!

Acknowledgments

And, as always, I am eternally grateful to my team of editors, Peter Keim and Lynn Mapp, my book cover designer, Lou Harper, and my narrator for Audible and iTunes, Angela Dawe. They are the people who take what I've written and help turn it into the book I proudly present to you, my readers! I also wish to thank my coffee group of writers who listen and encourage me to keep on going. Thank you, Peggy Staggs, Lynn Mapp, Cate Cobb, Nikki Jean Triska, Joanne Pence, Melanie Olsen, and Megan Bryce. And to you, my fabulous readers, I thank you for your continued support and encouragement. Without you, this book would not exist. You are the wind beneath my wings.

www.ingramcontent.com/pod-product-compliance
Lightning Source LLC
Chambersburg PA
CBHW022107240626
47153CB00007B/2262
* 9 7 8 1 9 6 2 4 5 2 8 9 2 *